"I have read Four Arrows' novel, *Last Song of the Whales*, and thank him for this most engaging presentation which can allow people to become aware of the critical marine conservation issues facing our world. Entertainment is a good way to educate people and this is what he is doing."

Francine Cousteau
President of the Cousteau Society

"The Ocean's Plastic Plague is doubling every decade with no end in sight. As a result, her creatures are suffering and dying in droves. Four Arrows offers the profound insight that only by realizing our true partnership with the most charismatic of sea creatures will a distracted humanity find the courage it needs to stop in its tracks to retool and redirect its destructive productivity."

Captain Charles Moore
Algalita Marine Research Foundation

"Four Arrows has, in his unique, artistic, open-hearted way, unearthed a metaphor of profound, biblical implications. One that affects the heart as deeply as it does the mind. This book may change the way the reader looks at the sea, and perhaps even the way all of us view the world."

Roger Wolfson
Television Writer and former U.S. Senate Staffer

"Last Song of the Whales is a both a tone poem and and an ecological treatise that takes the reader into a world of sensation and thought unlike any other. Some might call it imposssible...as improbable a story as the one about Men walking on the Moon would be to a Kogi tribesman from the remote mountains of Columbia.

"It is easy to suspend what we think to be true when Don 'Four Arrows' Jacobs speaks to us so convincingly about both the universal intelligence of our planet and the terrible state of our life support system. Thanks to Four Arrows for offering us another way and another reason to "Live Like We Love The Ocean."

Tim Dykman
Co-Director Ocean Revolution

Last Song of the Whales

Published in the USA by Savant Books and Publications
2630 Kapiolani Blvd #1601
Honolulu, HI 96826
http://www.savantbooksandpublications.com

Printed in the USA

Edited by Mary Yamin-Garone
Cover Art by Patrick Amos
Cover Design by Helen Babalis

10-digit ISBN: 0-9845552-5-0
13-digit ISNB: 978-0-9845552-5-3

Last Song of the Whales

Four Arrows

(D. T. Jacobs)

Savant Books
Honolulu, HI, USA
2010

Acknowledgement

First I would like to thank my wife for enduring the travails of being what she calls "a writer's widow" over the course of many years. Thank you, Beatrice Angela Jacobs, for this, for your help in editing and the many wonderful years of life together. I also wish to acknowledge my two grandsons, Kaien and Sage, and my daughter, Jessica, who continue to inspire my efforts to help our world regain its balance.

Because I wanted the imagined possibilities for the whales to be grounded in realistic possibilities, I solicited two of the world's foremost whale experts to answer many unusual questions during the writing of this book. Much appreciation goes out to Drs. Jonathon Stern and Jim Darling for their generosity and knowledge.

I want to mention my new friend, TV writer and ex-political speech writer, Roger Wolfson, whose passion for my story and creative ideas helped energize this project.

Thanks to Captain Charles Moore, one of the first to discover and write about the Pacific "garbage patch." He has dedicated his life to making the world aware of this problem. I hope this book will produce enough royalties to help support his Algalita Foundation and its important research.

My appreciation goes out to Jeanne Cousteau, widow of Jacques Cousteau and president of the Cousteau Foundation, for understanding the importance of this story.

Thanks to my editor, Mary Yamin-Garone, and my publisher, Daniel Janik. I would also like to thank Kelli Aspenleiter for her help in copy editing the final draft. And to Sue and Grant Bingham on whose boat, the Sedna, I encountered the humpback that inspired this story.

Special thanks to Patrick Amos, a Nuu-chah-nulth artist of the Mowachant-Muchalaht First Nations on Vancouver Island. He is a master carver in Cedar and ceremonial pieces for potlatches. He can be contacted at patrickamos@shaw.ca.

Finally, I wish to acknowledge the many non-human creatures, especially the whales, which are here to guide us if only we can recognize their wisdom.

I heard the song
Of the world's last whale
As I rocked in the moonlight
And reefed the sail,
It'll happen to you
Also without fail,
If it happens to me
Sang the world's last whale.

Last Song of the Whales

Four Arrows
(D. T. Jacobs)

Suddenly, he felt himself being sucked into a vortex. Light disappeared. A sensation of being lifted upwards quickly turned into a downward plunge. Pitch black darkness surrounded him as a powerful wave of water pushed him violently against something solid, something strange. He hit it hard, wrenching his shoulder. In the next moment he felt himself falling, not through water but air. He landed upon some great and soft thing. It gently pulled him backwards and enfolded him in a warm, fleshy mass. Unable to hold his breath any longer, and fully believing his death was imminent, he prepared to inhale whatever substance was waiting to enter his lungs. He had no hope for surviving.

1. The Jaws

Torrential rains and cold winds commenced their annual invasion of Salmon Beach Village. Brant Cormac and his wife, Angela, were now making fires in their stove every morning. Although they loved their home in Mexico as much as the one in British Columbia, November had come too quickly for them. Angela had booked reservations for the return flight to their winter home in Mexico. They were scheduled to take the ferry to the U.S. mainland the following day.

The village consisted of 10 dirt roads, each about a quarter mile long. More than 100 homes and an equal number of empty lots rested between Crown land and the ocean. The houses, a combination of shanties, old trailers and luxurious log cabins, crowded upon the shore in confusion, as if they had tumbled down drunkenly from the steep rainforest rising at the back. Most of them overlooked serene Barkley Sound to the south. Just to the east, around the end of a natural rock barrier, the often turbulent Pacific Ocean spread out to the west. All the homes were solar- or generator-powered and a well-protected boat ramp served the salmon fishing boats parked next to most of the homes.

From the nearby town of Ucluelet, 14 miles away via a bumpy, gravel road, several whale-watching businesses invited tourists from around the world to observe the gray whales, humpbacks, orcas, dolphins, seals and sea lions play and feed amidst the many islands of the Broken Group. The islands, a famous destination for kayakers, averaged less than half a mile across and were thick with cedar trees and bald eagles. Hundreds of them dotted the ocean as far as the eye could see. They were part of the largest area of ancient temperate rainforest left in British Columbia. More than 20 aboriginal tribes had thrived here for thousands of years, the highest concentration of First Nations on Vancouver Island. The few that remained, the Nuu-chah-nulth people, included small bands of the Ahousaht, Tlaoquiaht, Hesquiaht, Toquaht and Ucluelet.

A squall that looked like it would be an all-day event

disappeared as quickly as it arrived. In a short while, the sun had chased most of the clouds away. The ocean within the sound was calm, although it remained unfriendly in the unprotected seas to the west.

"Can you believe how beautiful it is today? I wish that we hadn't booked our flight back. What if it stays like this for a few more weeks? Besides, I'll bet it's going to be hot in Mexico when we get there." Brant knew he was begging for a fight.

"But we already booked the flight and we'll have to pay a penalty if we cancel. The weather here is sure to turn nasty soon. Don't be fooled by the sun. We'll be happy we left." Angela's reply showed no signs of the argument Brant expected.

"I don't know. We're all settled in here and…"

Angela interrupted him, knowing where he was going. "Don't do this, Brant. I know what you're thinking. It's neither the nice weather here nor the hot weather in Mexico that is causing you to change your mind. You just don't want to stop working on your book! Except for the few hours each day we are on the water, that's all you do. I'm a writer's widow again. You need a break from it and so do I."

Before retiring in frustration from his position teaching environmental science at the University of Arizona, Brant had written a number of textbooks. His motivation to write, although fueled by the "publish or perish" environment of his job, mostly reflected his desire, or perhaps his need, to promote Indigenous wisdom and its possibilities for addressing the world's ecological imbalances. Well, that was what he wanted to think he was doing anyway. Deep down he was trying to compensate for his identity crisis. His Cherokee mother had managed to keep him from appreciating any positive legacy from his Indian blood. Her own father had committed suicide and she wanted to protect Brant from the anti-Indian prejudice he apparently had suffered. Brant's childhood ritual of watching Saturday morning television reinforced his negative beliefs. He was 50 before he learned that Roy Rogers was also of mixed blood, a fact that might have changed his mind about always seeing the Indians as the bad guys.

In 1969, after serving in the Marine Corps during Viet Nam, Brant learned to reject a number of assumptions about the world he had come to believe. One of these was about the value of Indigenous Peoples. Eventually, he learned to cherish, rather than reject, aboriginal values. He had not managed to live his life—emotionally or physically—according to these values, such as living according to the idea that everything is interconnected, although he was trying to do so more and more.

"Yeah, you're probably right but I only need a few more weeks to get a handle on this book and I've got all these damned notes from those studies and I…" He knew his argument was weak so he stopped in mid-sentence. He was working on a book comparing neuropsychology with Indigenous beliefs, disagreeing with most of the Western scientific studies that concluded that generosity is self-serving, deception is an evolutionary survival skill and only human beings are capable of altruism.

"You don't need to be ruining your eyes any more with all this computer work. You're supposed to be retired. Besides, I'm not sure all this writing is doing anyone any good. The environment is worse than ever."

There it was—the fight Brant expected. Angela counter-punched and it landed below the belt.

"I mean, your book about what consuming shrimp is doing to the oceans didn't stop our friends from ordering shrimp cocktail the other night." Another low blow.

Brant was about to escalate the argument but stopped again. He knew she was right.

"OK, we'll stay on schedule for Mexico. What do you say we take advantage of this beautiful day? Let's see if Gilles and Sue want to go whale watching."

Brant had already stored their kayaks and sailboat for the winter but Gilles and Sue Bellingham's 16-foot aluminum fishing boat was ready to go and so were they. The friends and neighbors quickly prepared for a last tour of the Broken Group. Gilles gathered two crab traps and some frozen bait. Brant grabbed a new dry suit he wanted to test. They were on the water by noon.

Within minutes, the Broken Group Islands surrounded the little boat with their massive rock formations, primeval vegetation and towering trees. The craggy saw-toothed spires of the Mackenzie Range to the east loomed in the distance where the mainland curved around Toquart Bay to the south. Some spots of snow still appeared on the northern exposures and the sun bounced off the whiteness here and there, causing the volcanic basalts and breccias to glisten. From the nearby islands, steam lifted off the rainforest leaves, still wet from the recent precipitation.

Gilles turned on the VHF radio. Everyone listened to the transmissions between the whale-watching boats that shared sighting locations with one another. Although competitors, the boat operators already had their paid customers so they did their best to help each other. Today there were not only a few humpbacks in the area but several resident orcas from the north coast were visiting. They apparently were part of a larger group traveling toward southern California, a mysterious migration that had marine biologists baffled. They guessed that the whales were not getting enough chinook salmon to eat in their home grounds.

Just in front of the Stopper Islands—each of the islands or island groups had a name—Gilles slowed down the boat to toss out his two circular crab pots. He had brought two frozen salmon carcasses and the remains of one lingcod. The salmon were for the crabs but the lingcod was to entice the eagles to soar from their island tree perches so Angela could snap some photos. They were accustomed to folks feeding them and seemed to enjoy the free fish even if slightly frozen. After dropping the traps and marking the buoys' location with his GPS, Gilles accelerated through the smooth waters, looking for whales. Sue and Angela sat in front of the helm station, huddled close and bundled up like Eskimos. In spite of the warm sun, at about 20 mph the November ocean air was cold.

Gilles was at the helm behind the windshield with Brant sitting next to him. The wind blew a plastic bag past Gilles who grabbed it before it went overboard. He handed it to Brant who reached around and gave it to Sue. She in turn gave it to Angela, who put it where it was originally, tucked partially into her gym bag. A few minutes later another swirl of wind picked it up and the entire process repeated itself.

"How many times are we going to do this?" Gilles yelled jokingly over the noise of the 40 horsepower outboard.

"This proves that slapstick comedy is based on real life, eh?" Brant replied. "Honey, would you put the plastic in your gym bag so it doesn't blow overboard?" Brant and Angela both disliked seeing plastic in the ocean. They saw bird skeletons on the beach filled with plastic bags and bottle caps where their stomachs once were. Once they watched a sea lion pup strangled to death because its head was caught in a plastic six pack holder and they could not get close enough to cut it off.

Sue pointed toward an eagle sitting atop a tall cedar near the edge of David Island. Gilles maneuvered the boat as close to the rocks as possible and waved the lingcod remnants at the bird. Sue began chirping her eagle impersonation. Gilles then tossed the fish onto the rocks, moved offshore a bit and killed the motor while the group watched and waited. For some reason the eagle remained uninterested. Brant joked it was because Sue had said the wrong thing with her chirping. After about five minutes Gilles started the engine and moved on. Remarkably, the eagle followed, leaving the fish on the rocks. He soared downward and circled as if to say, "Thanks anyway," or "Have you got anything better?" before returning to his perch.

Twenty minutes later Gilles slowed down the boat again. Several hundred meters ahead the blow trail of a whale hovered above the water. The explosive exhalation out of its two blowholes lasted several seconds before a muscular flap resealed the openings. This created a large vapor column that rose at least 10 feet above the water and remained for 30 seconds. Then the whale submerged. Not knowing where it would appear next Gilles turned off the motor again.

The friends took turns betting on where the creature would surface next. No one was ever right. Once it "spy-hopped" 100 yards to the south. Like someone treading water, its huge bulky head was vertical while it scanned the sea for whatever reason. It stayed up long enough to expose the whitish throat grooves running down its chin. When it dove one of its flippers was revealed. Sue guessed the whale was 40-feet long and the flipper was at least 10-feet long.

A minute later the whale surfaced, this time less than 50 yards away. It exhaled loudly and slowly vanished again just after humping its back and exposing its short dorsal fin. Angela noticed the fin had a horseshoe shape, possibly caused by a large chunk being bitten out of the center by a killer whale. It was common to see such scars on the humpbacks. Five more minutes elapsed and no sighting. Perhaps the whale had moved on behind the nearest island. As Gilles was about to start the motor, a school of small fish jumped up in front of the boat, as if being chased by something. Moments later the whale resurfaced within a yard of the bow's port side! Sue screamed in surprise and Angela excitedly snapped a photo. The humpback hovered for at least four or five seconds, actually rubbing against the bottom of the boat. Although it looked black in the distance, up close it had a gray tint. Its dorsal fin was no more than a foot high, curving back toward the boat with the slight double-peaked notch on top.

To be this close to such a large and intelligent creature humbled all four passengers. It submerged and everyone stood in silence for a moment. Then, with wide grins, they slapped hands in celebration of this rare opportunity to have been so close to such a magnificent mammal.

The experience touched Brant deeply, more than he was prepared to share. Although this surprised him, he knew such feelings were common during whale encounters. Some people had written about a transfer of peaceful vibrations between humans and whales, referring to a kind of interspecies telepathic communication.

In fact, Brant was trying to communicate with the whale telepathically. He found himself inviting the whale to return. It all happened too fast and he knew he would likely never see a whale that close again.

"Can you believe it? He was right under the boat. I should have jumped on him!" Brant wasn't sure why he said that and was sorry he blurted it out.

"Sure and then we all would wind up in a Canadian prison," Gilles said in a serious tone.

Brant knew that Gilles was right. Mammal Protection Acts in both the U.S. and Canada strictly forbade "harassing" whales. Even playing music to them for experimental purposes was illegal. Hell, he taught this to his students. What was going on in his mind? Would he really have jumped on the whale's back? Sure, he had done some crazy things in his day, like when he accepted a dare to ride a bucking bronco in a backwater Missouri rodeo. Of course, he was a teenager then. Well, what the hell, maybe he would jump on a whale. Why not? Rather than retract his comment he announced emphatically, "Yep, if he comes back, I'm riding him!"

Brant spoke while he was changing into his dry suit. It came with an under suit made of synthetic material also designed to provide warmth and wick moisture away. Although the suit was difficult to get into, it was light and more comfortable than he had imagined. It even had a pee zipper for those times in the kayak when he would need to use a bottle.

After donning the suit he declared he was ready for the next whale. "OK, captain, find me that humpback to ride!"

The party continued to circle the eastern portion of the Broken Group. They spotted a spout more than a mile away but saw no other whales. A large sea lion did come close enough for Angela to take some photos. Brant was snacking on trail mix and beginning to think that putting on the dry suit was a bad idea. Gilles had been using the trolling motor and was slowly moving along the lee side of the islands. The sun was beating down on the black material of Brant's dry suit.

"Man, I'm getting hot. Do you mind if I take a dip? Good time to test this thing out." Gilles turned off the motor as Brant jumped into the calm waters. The suit's buoyancy caused his legs to want to float up and turn him sideways.

"Can you throw me the Kayak vest, honey?" Angela tossed it to him. He put on the life jacket and the problem was fixed.

"Wow, the suit sure keeps you warm. Can you believe it? It's like we are in a lake!"

Boating in the Broken Group between islands was indeed like being in a lake. The waters in the sound were significantly warmer than the open sea just a few miles to the west. An occasional bulb of kelp, a red and purple starfish on the rocks or a breaching whale quickly popped the illusion.

After a few more minutes of swimming and cooling off, Brant managed to climb back into the boat with some difficulty, using a portable ladder at the stern.

That's when it happened.

Angela saw it first. "Uh, guys, there is a whale next to the boat. He's just floating there looking at us." She spoke softly as if she didn't think the others would believe her. Unlike Brant, however, Angela wouldn't joke so all three immediately looked to see what she was looking at. The weight of the foursome standing on the boat's starboard side caused it to lean just enough to give everyone a perfect view of the humpback. It also frightened them into stepping back to the center. The whale's great head, dotted with barnacles and white circles where barnacles had been, floated on the surface with one eye studying the humans. After a short while in silence, the animal exhaled softly. The two couples winced joyfully at the smell of rotten fish and sea mud.

Without hesitation, Brant stepped up on the freeboard and swung his leg over the safety rail.

"Don't you dare!" Angela screamed.

Before Gilles could second Angela's order, Brant had gently stepped aboard the back of the whale and quickly positioned himself for its reaction. The whale moved forward several yards. Brant was riding a whale and could not contain his jubilance. He yelled out, "God, this is really happening!" Suddenly, the whale, with an amazing acrobatic action, propelled itself down into the green ocean waters. Brant stretched out on his stomach with his legs spread for balance. He clasped the barnacles, closed his eyes and held his breath, determined to make the ride last as long as possible.

The whale leveled off somewhere around 20 feet and swam parallel to the surface with an undulating motion that reminded Brant of an amusement park carousel creature. He looked up at the sun's rays filtering down toward him, the salt burning his eyes. He smiled at the incredible image of himself on the whale's back, flying through the ocean in the dim, shadowy liquid. He savored every feeling. It seemed like an eternity passed when he began to gasp for oxygen and realized he would have to let go.

Brant knew he would have no problem swimming the short distance to the top. He held his breath for as long as he could before standing and thrusting himself upwards. Within seconds he popped above the surface and took in as much air as possible. He was no more than 100 yards from the boat and he raised his arms to signal his position. He had ridden the whale and no one could take that away from him.

Suddenly he felt himself being sucked into a vortex. Light disappeared. A sensation of being lifted upwards quickly turned into a downward plunge. Darkness surrounded him as a powerful wave pushed him violently against something solid, something strange. He knew it was the baleen plates hanging from the upper jaw. He hit them hard, wrenching his shoulder. In the next moment he felt himself falling, through air, not water. He landed on top of some strange object. His first thought was of a giant leech. It gently pulled him backwards and enfolded him in a warm, fleshy mass. No longer able to hold his breath and fully believing his death was imminent, Brant prepared to inhale whatever substance was awaiting his lungs. He had no hope for survival.

Instead of fear, however, he felt an indescribable peace. He saw, even felt, a soft white light surrounding him. Friends and relatives, those who had passed away and those still living, were smiling at him lovingly. In another instant, former enemies appeared and Brant found himself shaking hands with them in mutual forgiveness. The whole time a beautiful, harmonic music rang in his ears.

As quickly as the tranquil images came, they disappeared when he realized he was not going to die. Fear now consumed him. At the same time he was amazed at having experienced such a wonderful calm when he was certain of his death. Brant, knowing he was on the whale's tongue, could not believe he was still alive. The whale dove deeper for a few seconds, then leveled off, perhaps rising a little as it moved along the horizon. Brant still was breathing in the foul-smelling but life-sustaining air.

Brant guessed he had been inside the humpback for 30 minutes. He was astounded that he was able to breathe while inside the creature's mouth. Several times the whale surfaced to breathe. Each time he heard, even felt, the animal's explosive exhale. At its peak the tongue tensed momentarily then relaxed until the whale's next breath. Brant took this all in, observing everything to avoid succumbing to his growing sense of claustrophobia.

Another 5 or 10 minutes elapsed and Brant was having difficulty breathing. Convinced that the trapped air was running out, he felt like he would suffocate. He could not imagine why the whale kept him in its mouth so long. Maybe the scientists were wrong about humpbacks having a small throat and not being able to eat mammals. Maybe they did not need teeth or a big passageway to their stomach. Maybe whales digested larger animals with their tongue before dismissing all of these ridiculous possibilities.

Suddenly his torture ended. The whale surfaced and opened its mouth wide enough for Brant to see daylight. It floated with its lower jaw just above the ocean's surface. Brant could barely see the hazy mountain shapes just east of Salmon Beach in the shadowy light cast by the setting sun. He figured he was at least 10 miles out to sea. In any case, this was Brant's chance to escape. Rescuers would easily find him if they had managed to follow the whale. If not, the salmon boats routinely went this far out to fish and he would not be too difficult to spot. The Coast Guard also probably had dispatched an airplane. With a hopeful heart he began maneuvering his way along the whale's tongue to the edge of the lower jaw. He could not negotiate the trip and constantly fell backwards. The effort was unnecessary, however, for the whale pushed him out into the ocean with a flick of its tongue. Brant landed hard in the water, injured from strains, cuts and bruises but alive. The whale looked at him and disappeared beneath the murky water.

Threatening skies hid the last rays of the disappearing sun. The menacing weather offered little reason for Brant to feel overly confident about his new situation. The wind was strong and his effort to ride the intense 10 to 12 feet high waves was exhausting him. Twenty minutes or so went by and he started vomiting. Between the waves and his motion sickness he struggled to keep the saltwater out of his mouth and nose. He appreciated the dry suit, booties and Kayak life vest. They were saving him from hypothermia as the waters here were much colder than in the sound. Although his hands and face were cold, he believed he could survive the storm until the next day when he surely would be rescued.

Last Song of the Whales

2. The Night

Brant's belief that he would survive diminished after several hours in the dark night and turbulent ocean. He was being tossed violently by the waves. The darkness obscured his ability to read them and forced him to swallow water each time a wave surprised him. He fought for every breath and the effort was exhausting. He was ready to give up the fight when he heard a motor.

He waited for the next wave to take him up to its crest then desperately searched in all directions before being dropped back down in the trough. Nothing. On the second lift he saw running lights illuminating what appeared to be a fishing boat about 100 meters away. It was attempting to tack back and forth across the northerly swells, aiming for the protection of the coastline less than an hour away. Brant could not imagine why the boat was out in this weather. Maybe the crew had gone too far out or spent too much time trying to bring in the "big one." Perhaps, he considered, they had been looking for him!

The craft was slowly making headway. One of the crew members was shining a floodlight in front of the boat, probably looking for drifting logs. Brant struggled to stay up on the crest of each wave for as long as possible, hoping the beam would land on him. He could see the name of the boat. The starboard bow running lights illuminated "Bella Bella." Now he could make out the man in the foul-weather gear holding the searchlight. He was attached to the boat with a harness and line. Suddenly the light beam blinded Brant for a moment before the waves moved him out of the way. Brant was sure the man saw him! At the peak of the next wave Brant screamed at the top of his lungs. Just before sinking back into the trough, however, he saw a maverick wave lift the boat wildly to starboard, flipping it up and over and smashing it upside down into the water.

Brant could not believe his eyes. It seemed like forever before another wave brought him up again so he could see what was happening. The boat lights were gone. Suddenly something hard came up against his feet. He thought perhaps he was over the wreckage until the object moved. His first thought was that it was a shark and the terror of this possibility made him forget the boat for the moment. A minute later he heard the familiar blow of a whale. The next instant the humpback took Brant into its jaws again, forced out the water as before, closed its mouth tight, and dove below the dangerous waves.

Brant felt a sense of security that contrasted with the first time the whale had snatched him up. He endured the darkness and even found himself clutching against the warm, almost hot, tongue until he stopped shivering. The loud wind, pelting rain and stifling saltwater were gone. So, too, were any concerns about sharks. He pressed his face and hands into the warm tongue like a baby clinging to its mother's breast.

Although relatively safe beneath the chaotic seas, Brant nonetheless vacillated between a sense of security and a feeling of horror. There were no words to describe the various versions of reality he was experiencing. Then, with no sense of how long he had been in its jaws, the whale spit him out. The storm had either subsided or the animal had taken him beyond it. He was greeted by smaller waves, less winds and intermittent starlight.

Brant floated in the sea for the rest of the night. At

long last, a fog swept gently in and he could see the sun struggling to appear. The whale was nearby. Its head was pointing down and it was uttering a haunting series of vocal transmissions that to Brant's conscious mind was an obvious effort to communicate. He had heard "whale songs" on recordings and at Sea World but none came close to what he was hearing now. There were similar moans, groans and whistles but the tones, inflections and intentionality left no question that the whale was talking to someone. Every note the whale uttered went to the core of Brant's being. The music consisted of two distinct but somewhat unrelated harmony lines, never interrupted by a pause for breathing,

Brant knew whale experts claimed that humpbacks sang to court a mate, to navigate or to threaten competitors but the singing he was hearing seemed to relate to none of these things. The sound began as a low-pitched lion roar followed by a high-pitched soprano vibration that ended with a rising tone, like humans used when asking a question. The low-pitched words or notes made up one phrase while the higher frequency notes created a different one. The whale repeated this composition for about 20 minutes. It culminated in a final theme that revealed a more passionate expression. The whale repeated its unique sound for an hour until he began to slap his tail and let out a series of newer, more enthusiastic sounds. It accelerated forward, rolled and slapped its tail again, its full body out of the water.

After frolicking this way the whale swam back to Brant, looking at him as if to ask why he wasn't having fun. In spite of the remarkable show that only a day before would have awed him, Brant no longer wanted to be part of it. His second wind was disappearing as he began to dry heave. His little folly was now a huge disaster for himself and others who were now no doubt looking for him. The saltwater mixed with his tears as he thought about his wife, Angela.

Last Song of the Whales

3. Rescue Efforts

Angela was the first to see Brant when he surfaced and began waving his hands.

"There he is! He's OK," she cried with relief. "Oh my God, oh no, the whale…" she stopped in mid-sentence. She saw the whale take Brant into its mouth. She had no doubt. Gilles had been starting the motor and missed it, although it was obvious to him that Brant was no longer in sight. Sue saw the whale but didn't see Brant waving in the water. It all happened too fast.

Gilles started the outboard and sped toward where Brant had been. All three were beside themselves trying to comprehend what happened. Gilles knew the whale could stay underwater for 40 minutes and could travel 16 miles in that time. If he had taken Brant…no, it wasn't possible. Something else must have happened. Maybe the whale knocked him out and he got caught in a current that was holding him down. Gilles picked up his VHF radio and turned to channel 16.

"Mayday…Mayday…Mayday. This is the small fishing boat, *Sedna*. We are located in the Broken Group of Islands with a man overboard. Stand by for GPS coordinates!"

While he was pressing buttons on his dash-mounted GPS keyboard, Gilles received a response to his emergency call. "This is the Coast Guard Radio Ucluelet. Please switch to channel 16 Alpha. We are enroute to your area. ETA is two-zero minutes." To make it from the Coast Guard station to the boat's location in 20 minutes they would likely be using their Zodiac Hurricane.

Gilles switched to the new channel and gave his coordinates several times. "Repeat, the *Sedna,* 16-foot aluminum boat. We are at Latitude 48.85 North and Longitude 125.38 West." Gilles had kayaked the area for years and wanted to say which island he believed they were near but what if he was wrong? The coordinates were best for describing his location anyway.

Angela was looking through the binoculars desperately, occasionally brushing tears from the eyepiece. Sue was dwelling on the mention of the boat's name, *Sedna*. She never thought they would use it on the radio like this. She was thinking of the irony. *Sedna* was an Inuit goddess of the underworld and goddess of the marine mammals.

Within the hour several fishing boats from Ucluelet Harbor and Toquart Marina were attempting to find a "man overboard" in a black dry suit. Gilles kept his boat at their original location on orders from the Coast Guard. The others spread out around the nearby islands and along the Imperial Channel all the way to the open ocean. Some had gone into the rough seas. The strong, outgoing tide might have brought a man that far. The Coast Guard had two helicopters engaged in the search, a Bell 212 and a Sikorsy S61-N. The Coast Guard had not revealed Angela's claim about the whale having taken the man. No one was looking for a whale.

Angela had been clear about seeing the whale take Brant away but the radio traffic kept referring to a "man overboard." She angrily asked Gilles for the radio, grabbing it before he could ask why.

"Hello. I am the wife of the man you are trying to find. Please listen to me! We SAW a humpback whale take my husband into its mouth! We have to find the whale. It has a notched fin. It can't be that far away. Please!"

Gilles interrupted her and gently but firmly took the radio from her hands. "We need to keep the channel open," Gilles explained.

Still in shock, Sue managed to support her friend's conviction. "What if the whale does still have him?"

Gilles obviously had been thinking about that, too.

"Then what? Even if they find the same whale do we want them to kill it and cut it open? There probably are half a dozen still here and they all probably have bites out of their fins. Besides, I don't think anyone believes it. Humpbacks don't eat people. If that is what happened to Brant he would be the first to say we should not kill a whale to find his body!"

Angela knew Gilles was right.

Ninety minutes had passed since Brant disappeared with the whale. The Coast Guard was announcing a weather warning over the radio. A squall was moving in fast with possible gale force winds. The transmission was barely over when the sky blackened. Gilles immediately headed toward the boat ramp. Presumably the other craft also headed for home. Angela could not believe that people would even consider stopping the search because of a weather warning, let alone Gilles. By the time they reached the ramp, the storm hit. The boat ramp was extremely well protected from wind and waves but it was all Sue and Angela could do to hold the boat in place while Gilles got the truck. She knew there was no choice but to quit until the storm subsided.

Gilles and Sue brought Angela to their home, stopping by her house on the way to pick up Zorro, the Cormac's Mexican Chihuahua. Angela caressed the dog, crying and telling it what happened to its master. Brant had always owned big dogs, never understanding what people saw in such "useless" little things. He loved the little guy, however, and realized how wrong he had been. Against his own orders he even allowed Zorro to sleep with them every night. The little dog seemed to understand that something terrible had happened. With Angela's face close to his, he licked her tears away.

Sue and Angela drank coffee inside the Bellingham's small cabin, watching the storm's fury. Zorro was huddled in Angela's lap. Gilles made a fire in the stove and stooped to pet the dog. "That thunder sounds like two old dogs growling, doesn't it, Zorro?"

Then all eyes looked toward the VHF radio Gilles had placed on the table. "This is the Bella Bella. We are about 20 miles southwest of Sail Rock in the middle of this storm. We are making some headway but it is tough. We all have our French harnesses on and attached to the boat. Someone please tell my wife we are OK. Why we are still out here is a long story. We'll let you know if we decide to turn and head southwest for the islands. Let's hope not. Over."

In spite of the considerable static Gilles recognized John Huffington's voice. He owned the Bella Bella, a 29-foot Trophy with twin 250 Suzuki Motors. He was a good captain and an avid fisherman. Gilles was curious as to why they were late coming in. He put on his raincoat and drove the truck over to the Huffington's cabin to tell her about her husband's transmission. She did not have a radio and would be worried.

Gilles' house was only a few blocks from the Huffington cabin where John's wife, Marleen, lived. Gilles took his time driving, however, for the dirt roads were slippery and the rain was almost horizontal. He heard the roar of the ocean before he started the engine. He would not want to be out there tonight, not in a boat, not in the ocean or... He caught himself before he said not in a whale.

Last Song of the Whales

4. The Day After

With Zorro still sleeping under the blankets at her feet, Angela woke reaching for Brant. Pulling his pillow to her breasts, she remembered. Dream memories were quickly overshadowed by a cascade of thoughts. She tried her best to stop them and recall her dream. What was it she saw? Something glowing in the darkness like green diamonds. There was a large wing or perhaps a dinosaur's tail flapping through it and with each flap the light got brighter. Then her memory of the dream vanished. She looked out the window. The storm had receded but the atmosphere remained ominous. An alder branch that broke off during the night stretched across the deck. A light fog was managing to keep the sun at bay. Angela felt a baleful energy as if some conquering army had made its way into the village and was resting for a while before it began to rape and pillage.

Having no phone at the cabin, she had been unable to contact friends and relatives about Brant. This morning she planned on driving to the Coast Guard station in Ucluelet to be sure they were continuing the search. She hoped no trees were down across the road. If so it would be days before anyone got to them. In town she would call everyone starting with his sister in St. Louis. Brant and Angela had no children. An emergency operation relating to an early pregnancy issue had ended the idea but both of them also had been reluctant to bring a child into the world for other reasons.

She arrived in town before 6:45 a.m. and stopped briefly at the Whaler's Café. She ordered a scone and hot herbal tea to go.

"You're comin' down from Salmon Beach, aren't ya?" asked the person behind the counter. She was a buxom woman, probably in her 40s. Her hair looked like it spent more time on the open sea than in the café. Her cheery disposition, windburned cheeks and strong hands supported the assumption. Indeed, she was Jodi Marin, Captain of the Orca, one of the whale-watching boats owned by the same people who owned the coffee shop. The offices were next door and from her vantage point

Angela could see racks of orange foul-weather suits of various sizes.

Angela nodded. She had no energy to talk and was afraid if she did she would start crying again.

"Heard it was a bad night up your way. Did ya hear about the fellow they say was taken by a humpback? Don't believe it myself. Been out there watchin' 'em for 30 years, since I was in high school. No way. Couldn't fit a volley ball in its esoph. Somethin' happen though. Heard the guy rode it first. Don't believe none of it. Served him right if he did. It's 'ginst the law, you know. Still, sounds like the guy wasn't found so that ain't good. An if that weren't bad enough, John Huffington's boat never made it in last night. They ain't been found either. His brother-in-law and some other guy. I think they went way out there to get some halibut. Bet he landed a big one, didn't want to let it go and didn't think the storm a hit so quick-like."

Angela paid, and, feeling her eyes welling up again, .she drove to the Coast Guard, determined to stay on task. Were they heading out to look for the whale at first light? If not, why not? She had her digital camera. They could take her photos and magnify the whale's image. She was sure it would show the notched fin.

The two crew members manning the desk assured her the operation was scheduled to continue throughout the day once the fog cleared some more. They not only were looking for her husband but also for three other men whose boat may have sunk in the same area. She couldn't go with them but she could call the station for updates any time.

"I'm so sorry about these men. I really am, but why isn't anyone listening to me? A whale took my husband and I think it still has him. I know it doesn't make sense but does it make sense that a man wearing a rubber suit and life jacket can't be found in Barkley Sound?"

The junior officer, a young, stocky man with a bandaged hand, who looked like he had been living off the sea his whole life, gently replied, "Ma'am, it was a hell of a storm last night. We're afraid the current took him out of the sound and the wind and waves took him further out to sea. With the way the waves have been and probably will be today, it's like looking for a needle in a haystack. I'm so sorry, ma'am. We are doing our best. I promise you. As for the whale, I believe you. I really do. If you saw the whale take him then it did. But what did it do with him? It had to spit him out. So then we are back to having to look for the man, not the whale. See what I mean? We're doing it right. You have to trust us."

Angela thanked the man and went to the public telephone outside the Crow's Nest Laundromat. She had a jar full of loonies and toonies, the Canadian terms for one and two-dollar coins. She began the agonizing process of calling friends and relatives in the U.S. and Mexico. Repeating the story was as difficult as watching it. She had to compose herself before calling Allen Wayne in Vancouver. Allen was a colleague of Brant's who taught in the University of British Columbia's Environmental Sciences program.

"Allen. It's Angela Cormac, Brant's wife."

"What a surprise! Are you two in Mexico?"

"Allen, something awful happened. We're still here. We were whale watching yesterday and a humpback came right up next to us. Brant jumped on it and rode it for a while."

"He did what?!" Allen interrupted.

"After he fell off, the whale turned back on him and took him in its mouth. I saw it. Search and Rescue looked for Brant's body for a few hours before the storm hit.

They think he is in the water. He was wearing a dry suit and a life jacket. They are going to look for him today but not the whale. I think he is still with the whale and no one will believe me." She started to cry.

"Oh, my God, Angela. Listen, honey, we'll all be laughing about this soon. Whales just don't eat people. I mean, it wasn't a killer whale was it?"

"No. It was a humpback and I saw it take Brant into its mouth with my own eyes. I saw it but no one believes me. I don't know if the whale is a year-round resident or one that migrates but I need to find out. I know Brant is alive. I can feel it."

"How can I help? Do you want to come and stay with us? We have plenty of room and..."

"No, thank you, Allen. I have to stay here. Like I said, they are going to continue the search soon. But I do need a favor. I want to talk to a humpback whale expert. Does UBC have any good marine biologists who would be willing to talk to me?"

"Honey, I don't know anyone off hand. But you know we do have a highly respected facility where they study whales. It's called the Marine Mammal Research Unit. Just a second. I can give you the number."

Allen gave her the number of MMRU's switchboard. Angela wrote it down and promised to keep Allen updated. Then she dialed the number.

"Marine Mammal Research. How can I direct your call?"

"I want to talk to someone who knows about humpbacks," Angela replied. The secretary transferred her call to Professor Larry Stetman.

"Hello. This is Dr. Stetman."

Angela repeated her story. The professor told her he studied sea lions and the only faculty researching whales that specialized in humpbacks retired a few years ago. He suggested she contact Loni Stern. Last he heard she was at the University of Hawaii. She knew more about humpback whales from B.C. to Maui than anyone except for the Nootka Indians.

Angela thanked him and hung up. She then went to the Ucluelet First Nations Museum. She had heard that a Nootka woman from nearby displayed her artwork there. Nootka was an Anglo version of what the people called themselves, Nu-chah-nulth, which translates to "along the mountains." Brant had told her not to call the Indians around here Nootka. It was an offensive term, he said, like calling the Lakota "Sioux," which was French for snake.

An elderly woman, with age lines chiseled into her face by the sun, sat in a beautiful rocking chair decorated with the typical geometric shapes and symbols of the Pacific Northwest aboriginals. The walls were cluttered with beautiful carvings, colored mostly with reds, blacks, whites and yellows. There was an organic feeling that set the objects apart from the art in most non-Indian galleries. Most of the items served as a means of transmitting wisdom, not entertainment, although now art had become one of the few ways for its creators to earn a living.

The energy in the place combined with that of the old woman's vibrations soothed Angela's nerves and helped contain her emotion. After a friendly exchange about the weather Angela introduced herself. The woman reciprocated and offered her hand. Her name was Evelyn, she said, with the accent of a Native speaker coupled with the uplifting tones typical to a western Canadian's speech.

"Are you Evelyn R. Walker, the painter?" Angela asked, knowing that if so she was talking to one of the most famous Nu-chah-nulth artists in British Columbia. Her work hung in the Royal Museum in Victoria and Angela was a fan, though she never could have afforded any of it.

The woman nodded and smiled. Her smile revealed warmth, compassion, and understanding in a way that made Angela want to spend the day with her.

"I am looking for someone who knows about humpback whales, someone who can tell me whether one might take a man into its mouth and carry him out to sea —if this is even possible—or if it's ever been done before."

Evelyn smiled again. This time her smile was more secretive as if remembering some joyful childhood experience. Angela guessed she was not thinking about the question as much as the idea of such a partnership between a man and a whale, one she seemed familiar with.

"Oh sure. Some of us used to hunt them, aye? My daddy and his daddy for as long as we have been. Not any more. But then those people, the whales, they fed us and gave us our light. They were our teachers, aye."

Angela looked around the room and noticed the many

wood carvings and totems depicting the humpback. "What do these whales symbolize?" She felt the question was too personal, too "new age" sounding. Brant would not have liked her asking it. She also felt she was getting off track from her mission but Evelyn did not seem concerned at all.

"They represent death and rebirth but maybe not like you think of these ideas. The humps teach us to remember who we really are, aye? They remind us that we, too, are creative, spiritual and intuitive beings and we go about the cycles of life and death, same as they do. Course, nowadays, they are trying to wake us up fore it is too late, aye."

"Wake us up? Too late? What do you mean?"

Evelyn smiled a third version of her smile. This one conveyed to Angela a contentment that somehow she had given Angela what she needed and that she had no more to say. She understood she never would get a direct answer from any of the elders about whether a humpback could have taken a human into its jaws. She gently shook Evelyn's hand, thanked her and turned to walk out the door. Before she reached it Evelyn spoke again.

"It is good if you pray for your husband, aye?"

Angela wanted to ask her how she knew. Instead she nodded and left.

It was around 10:30 in the morning when she left the museum. The fog was still in. She went back to the Coast Guard station and learned that the planes were scheduled to go up at noon, when the fog would not present a hazard. The crew on duty assured her that everything possible was being done to find her husband and the missing Bella Bella crew. From there, Angela went to the library to use the computer. She easily found Dr. Loni Stern's e-mail address and wrote:

Dear Dr. Stern:

Yesterday my husband, Dr. Brant Cormac, retired from the University of Arizona, was taken away by a humpback whale amidst the Broken Island Group on the west coast of Vancouver Island. The Coast Guard is searching for his body today. No one believes I saw the whale take him in its mouth. I was told you study these whales. This one has a horseshoe-shape notch in the middle of its dorsal fin. Can you tell me if it is a resident whale or if it migrates?

Please help me. I know my husband is still alive. I think the whale has him somehow. If I know the whale is a resident then our search should be within the hundreds of islands here. If the whale has left the area we should search the open ocean. Knowing this would be extremely helpful.

It also is important for me to know if it is possible for a man to survive for a short while in the mouth of a humpback.

Sincerely,

Angela Cormac

Angela read the letter to herself. Reading it made her want to tear it up. Now she understood why everyone thought her ideas were outlandish. Nonetheless she trusted her intuition. She knew what she saw. She hit the send button. Then Angela Googled, "Can a humpback whale take a man in its mouth?" She found nothing useful. There was one short story about a boy that was almost sucked into the mouth of a whale and a number of religious blogs and websites trying to convince people the Biblical story about Jonah and the whale was true. She printed one of them. Maybe, she thought, the Biblical scholars, an oxymoron Brant used to say, somehow got this one right. Suddenly she realized how desperate she was. The piece read:

Scientists are claiming that what witnesses saw with their own eyes cannot be true. This is more proof that people are not willing to learn from God's book. The fact is the record clearly states that, "God prepared a great fish to swallow up Jonah (1:17)." Disbelief that the man could have been swallowed smacks of an atheistic mentality. For years people have scoffed at the Biblical story, saying it is "impossible" and "therefore the Bible cannot be trusted." Not only is a whale's belly large enough to hold a man inside but many accounts similar to the Biblical account of Jonah have been recorded in recent years. In the late 1920s a seaman was swallowed by a large sperm whale in the vicinity of the Falkland Islands. After three days he was recovered unconscious. We must remember to trust the Bible first and foremost even if no other supporting evidence exists. If witnesses saw the whale swallow the man it is wrong on many levels to reject this possibility.

Angela had 10 minutes left on the timer for her computer and someone was waiting in line. She continued scanning the Google references and then, to her amazement, she found an article about Brant in the

Monday, November 9, 2010, online edition of the *Seattle Times*. She printed it quickly and left for the Coast Guard office.

Man Missing Off West Coast Vancouver Island—Possibly Taken by Whale

By Sam A. Chester, *Seattle Times staff reporter*

A Canadian Coast Guard search was temporarily suspended last night for a university professor, who witnesses say was taken by a 40-44-foot humpback whale. According to unnamed sources, the whale may have swallowed the man after he attempted to ride it.

According to a Coast Guard spokesperson from Ucluelet, two helicopters and an HC-130 Hercules aircraft searched the waters surrounding Barkley Sound yesterday afternoon on the west coast of Vancouver Island. They were looking for the professor and three crew members of a 29-foot fishing boat that may have gone down in a storm last night. The search is scheduled to continue today.

This morning sea conditions for the search indicate 23 mph winds with seas up to eight feet. Skies were overcast. This time of year the sea temperature can be as low as 40 degrees.

Sam Paulson, an expert on whales and dolphins at the Zoological Society of London, reported in the *London Guardian* that, "It would be very unlikely that a humpback would swallow an adult human owing both to the small opening to the esophagus and to it being primarily a plankton and small fish predator. If the whale took the man in its mouth, which certainly is large enough to hold a man, it would have spit him out immediately."

None of the names have been disclosed at this time, according to Richard Crews, Canadian Coast Guard spokesperson.

After reading and printing the news article, Angela copied and pasted it into a second e-mail to Loni Stern.

Last Song of the Whales

5. The Lesson

The whale continued looking at Brant then gracefully repeated its acrobatic routine. It nudged Brant several times when it returned. He felt like a mouse being toyed with by a cat. The whale was obviously not intending any harm. It seemed to want to play with him but was disappointed in Brant's attitude and his inability to have fun. Once in a while the whale would put its head underwater and resume the amazing calls. All this went on as the sun attempted to break through the light fog covering the ocean. Brant was getting cold again and the nausea was returning as he floated up and down on eight- or nine-feet high waves. He could not believe his thoughts. He was almost hoping he could go back into the whale's warm mouth. Almost.

Another hour went by with Brant watching the whale play, sing and apparently communicate with some distant listener. Suddenly Brant felt himself being lifted out of the water on the whale's back. Then it swam forward, undulating its flukes and powerfully propelling its large body to at least 15 mph. Because the waves were still high, the motion forced Brant underwater for 10 to 20 seconds every few minutes. Brant was about to jump off to keep from drowning but thought better of it. Better to be with the whale than alone in the vast ocean.

The sense of disbelief once again permeated Brant's thoughts. Here he was in the ocean, miles away from land, riding a whale! No movie, not even *Whale Rider*, a film Angela and he had rented recently, could be as fantastic. Brant, if he was right, was being carried across the ocean to Hawaii!

The whale stopped and floated on the surface, allowing Brant to breathe normally and relax his grip. The sun appeared and the whale seemed to be basking in it. Brant stretched out on its huge back and did the same. The swells were now only around five or six feet and far enough apart to not be so unpleasant. The pair floated quietly in silence.

Early afternoon was approaching. The sun was burning Brant's balding head. The salt was stinging his cuts and scrapes and his shoulder ached. The whale, apparently done napping, executed his vertical maneuver and scanned the horizon. This caused Brant's entire body to skid backwards all the way to the dorsal fin. He grabbed it just in time to keep from falling off. The animal then slapped the ocean with its tail, which flipped Brant into the water. The whale came up underneath him and lifted him again from just behind the dorsal fin where Brant had been moments before. The whale slapped his tail loudly again. In the distance Brant could see other whales coming toward them from the northeast.

Fifteen minutes later the whale, whom Brant referred to as "Boy," guessing he was a young male, met up with four other humpbacks—a mother with a calf and two adult male escorts. The creatures exchanged what seemed to be an enthusiastic greeting. Even if it was possible for Brant to avoid anthropomorphizing, he would have known the whales were happy to see one another. Boy seemed exceptionally pleased to greet the calf. While at first glance it appeared to be a first-time meeting the two immediately started playing as if the older whale was a long-lost uncle.

Brant went overboard into the cold ocean on the first

roll that Boy executed.

While he floated on the waves, the largest of the whales, 10 feet longer than Boy, approached Brant and studied him. The other adult whales soon followed. All of them began nudging him with their immense heads. Brant felt like a rag doll in the hands of giant children. The whales almost crushed him several times. Once a long pectoral fin scraped his left leg, shredding his suit even more and causing him to bleed. The whales noticed the blood and backed off. Boy ended his visit with the calf and intervened, or so it seemed, on Brant's behalf. After several vocal exchanges, Boy lifted the man up on his back and the group headed west. Again Brant held on for dear life as he was tormented by the water and cold. If the seas were flatter, Brant thought, it would have been easier to keep his head and face out of the water.

An intense hour or so elapsed. Brant was exhausted and felt he would have to let go. Boy slowed down enough for Brant to look around. A group of killer whales, including several mothers with calves and at least six adult males, were circling the humpbacks. They had approached from the east and probably were near the outside range of their Canadian turf. One of the orcas was about 27-feet long. It had a white hourglass marking behind its six-foot long dorsal fin. Twice as fast as the humpbacks, it managed to separate the 15 foot humpback calf from its mother while several orcas kept the other humpbacks at bay. The one with the hourglass suddenly came at Boy from the left side, mouth open. It was a harrowing sight for Brant to behold. The large jaws and sharp teeth were heading right for his leg. Brant was just about to jump off to the right to avoid being eaten when Boy turned quickly. The orca bit Boy on its neck five feet in front of Brant before turning away. Brant saw the results. There were six 10-inch strips of white blubber on Boy's neck but no sign of blood.

Boy did not flinch. He did slow down, however, to stay as close to the calf as possible. Brant noticed that none of the humpbacks were taking any evasive or defensive action. While the adult orcas maneuvered to keep the adult humpbacks away from the humpback calf, the three orca females and their calves surrounded it. The killers swam quickly in circles around it. The adults continued the circle but the orca calves, prodded by the adults, dove continually at the youngster and bit it. Pieces of blubber and skin spread out in all directions. Soon frigate birds appeared out of nowhere. They darted in and out, picking up the pieces of fat and swallowing them in hurried delight. Brant watched it all, both mortified and fascinated.

The attack ended as fast as it began. The humpback calf, not seriously injured, returned to its mother and the four humpbacks closed into a tighter formation. The orcas did not go away. Instead, they swam alongside the group of humpbacks with the strange human amidst them.

The orcas continued looking at Brant. At first he was worried they were coming for him. It would be easy to snatch him from Boy's back. He was, after all, the same size as their favorite prey, the harbor seal. After a while Brant dismissed the concern. Something told him not to worry. The violence against the calf was over for now. After 20 or 30 minutes the orcas split off and headed back east.

Several hours after the orcas departed, the sun began rolling slowly below the horizon. A line divided the sky in two. Above, it was slate gray with brown tones and not a cloud in sight. The other half, farther to the west, included the line of the horizon. It was rose-colored and strewn with wisps of dark clouds that stretched from the far line to the closer one. The horizon blurred into the undulating carpet of reddish brown water that made its way to Brant and the whales.

Brant looked down at the water. It was dark red. Marine scientists were not calling such seas "red tides" anymore. Instead they referred to them as "HABs," or "harmful algae blooms." HABs were increasing in the world's oceans and many other places, causing a decrease in the water's oxygen. New species of algae that did well without normal amounts of oxygen were proliferating and competing with one another by seeing which one could produce the most toxic excretions. Brant shivered as the sun disappeared. He was losing strength. He was ready to let go when he realized he was surrounded by jellyfish, another creature that did well in oxygen-deprived waters.

Last Song of the Whales

6. The Whale Expert

Loni Stern was an anomaly in whale research circles. She didn't seem to take herself too seriously. Always joking, never caring about academic turf wars, publishing or fame. She just loved her work. Once she was on an important research assignment at sea. She was scheduled to report her findings to representatives of the International Whaling Commission via the wireless communication on the boat. Thinking the radio had lost its transmission, or at least claiming so later, she began narrating her research conclusions in the voices of Walter Cronkite, Jacques Cousteau and a variety of cartoon characters. That act, combined with outspoken criticism of the Commission the year before, didn't sit well with the American Cetacean Society. The nonprofit group was sponsoring her current research.

Loni also had been less than diplomatic in

challenging the pro-whaling nations that were scapegoating whales for the worldwide decline in fish stocks. She had done this in person the previous May at the IWC conference in Anchorage. The Japanese delegates walked out of the meeting before she finished her tirade. Later they formally rescinded their invitation to hold the annual meeting in Yokohama the following year.

Most people tolerated, and many enjoyed, her eccentric personality. All understood she was the world's foremost expert on humpback whales. Some of her colleagues and students claimed she could identify individual animals by the unique scent coming from a blowhole. She also was proving that whales had a lot to teach humans about ecological systems. In fact, she was working on proving that these creatures might reveal more about our environment than we want to know!

A Canadian who did her undergraduate work in New Brunswick, Loni got her first name from her Hawaiian father, who passed away in 1976 when she was nine. He died just as whaling was winding down and serious whale research was beginning. She barely knew him. She hadn't set foot on the islands until she ran away from home at

16. Loni went to live with her father's sister for several years until she returned to Canada to get her degree. By the time she was 26 she had earned a double doctorate from the University of Hawaii: one in comparative psychology, the other in marine biology. Both specialized in marine mammals. At 30 she supervised marine mammal and coral reef studies in Hawaii, Japan and elsewhere in the Pacific. She was appointed research associate at the Kewalo Basin Marine Mammal Laboratory in Honolulu. Now, at 42, she had authored two books on humpback whales and numerous peer-reviewed articles. She also had presented at more professional workshops than she cared to remember. Although she commuted to the main campus to teach a graduate class for the University of Hawaii in Honolulu, most of her university work involved her time with the Pacific Whale Foundation not too far from her Maui home.

The day Angela sent her e-mail message to Loni the biologist was presenting at the Ritz-Carlton in Kapalua to a standing-room-only group at the fifth annual Whale Quest event. She spoke here often since she lived nearby in a small cottage located between Paia and Ho'okipa. An attractive woman with the gift of gab, people loved to hear Loni present. Her audience was laughing at the names she gave some of the whales whose photographs were being projected on a large screen. They were mostly names of aging rock stars. She was about to describe a new surface-based photographic identification technology called "D-tag." This was a noninvasive tag developed by the Woods Hole Oceanographic Institute that could be affixed to a whale's body with suction cups and record sound and movement far below sea level.

The audience was laughing when Loni's assistant handed her a page he had printed from the local online news forum, *Kapalua News*. It also was published as a monthly gazette with a distribution of about 140. The Kapalua Resort produced it to promote their business. Just below an advertisement that read, "Pick Your Passions at Kapalua Spa," the assistant, a 22-year-old student of Loni's named Akamu, an Indigenous Hawaiian working on his doctorate, had circled the following sentence. *"Keep your eyes open for a humpback whale with a notch in its dorsal fin, folks. One was reported having swallowed a professor in British Columbia yesterday and they might be heading our way!"* After

Loni read it she caught Akamu's eyes, gave him a puzzled stare and shrugged her shoulders. Akamu simply shrugged back.

Later that evening, barefoot and drinking her favorite concoction of rum, blue curacao, fresh pineapple juice and fresh coconut water, she turned on the computer to check her e-mail. While driving home she had wondered about the source of the tasteless attempt at a joke by the *Kapalua News* editor. Now she was reading the e-mail from the man's wife! Of course the woman was incorrect about the whale taking the man in its mouth. Maybe she was overly distraught and rationalizing some story instead of believing her husband drowned while near a whale. Even if a humpback had miraculously taken a man inside its mouth, something she supposed was theoretically possible, it would have spit him out soon after. It also was possible that her letter was a joke and so was the blurb in the *Kapalua News*.

Loni sent the woman a brief response. She said it was unlikely that a whale had her husband. As to whether a person could survive inside a humpback's mouth, she had never thought about it. It was certainly a large enough space. If the whale was intentional about it, that is, if it really wanted to make sure air and not water remained in its mouth so the man could breathe, there probably would be enough air for the man to live for a while. Regarding identification, it would be impossible for her to say whether a particular whale with a notch in its fin was a migrating whale or not. There were just too many whales. She was sorry she could not be of further help.

After she sent her reply she noticed another e-mail from Angela. She opened it and read the article from the Seattle newspaper. Now Loni knew it was not a joke. She went back and re-read Angela's first e-mail. Well, she thought, stranger things have happened. She could not imagine what good it would possibly do but she wrote another letter. Perhaps, as the woman suggested, she could find something that might help. She began typing:

Dear Mrs. Cormack:

I have reconsidered what I said in my last e-mail. If it will possibly help find your husband, I will ask my assistant to see if we know of any whales with the notch in the dorsal fin that you describe. If you have any photos they would help us match up with our own. Most of our 350 identification pictures, however, are of the underside of the fluke. It is unique, like a fingerprint. Did you happen to notice the markings under the fluke or the whale's tail?

We have tagged a dozen of our Hawaiian whales. Only half of them would likely be heading back here from Canada. Please understand that there are an estimated 20,000 humpbacks in the North Pacific waters. Any one of them might have visited Barkley Sound in November.

There is some good news. Only between 10 and 20 would reside in Vancouver Island's coastal waters. Let's see if we can determine if your whale is there.

I am deeply sorry for this tragedy. I will pray for your husband's safe return.

Sincerely,

Loni Stern

Last Song of the Whales

7. The Thirst

Being in the ocean surrounded by algae blooms and jellyfish was not a pleasant thought but Brant could not hold onto Boy any longer. Exhausted, he finally let go and the whale swam out from under him. The ocean waves were smoothing out. Darkness was coming fast and the first stars appeared. Brant figured his clothing would prevent stings unless, of course, he got hit in the face. In any case, he hoped Boy would come back. Hypothermia would take him by morning if a shark didn't.

It had been a little more than 24 hours since he had been on Gilles' boat. He did not remember drinking anything since breakfast. Brant's thirst was intense. He had gone a day without liquids before but the exertion, sun and saltwater were taking their toll. He licked his parched lips and unsuccessfully tried to draw moisture into his throat from the recesses of his mouth. He could feel his body mass shrinking with each breath. The salt from the sea and air and that which he'd swallowed accidentally chased away whatever water remained for normal metabolic functions. Soon his overworked blood cells would carry toxic urea to his kidneys. Even if he survived the cold, in another day the dehydration cycle would likely kill him.

In the meantime, Boy had dove and circled behind Brant as soon as Brant slid off. Still contemplating his fate, Brant nearly jumped out of his skin in surprise when Boy came at him from behind.

The whale lifted Brant onto its back again. This time, however, Brant was not high on the neck but rather just behind the dorsal fin. He laced his cold fingers together, locking them in place around the base of the fin. He relaxed his body, stretching his legs behind him. As the whale started swimming Brant felt the accentuated undulation of the tail moving. Now he could use the fin to keep his head above water, at least more often than before. He also did not have to use such strength and balance to stay in place.

Boy continued until he caught up with the other

whales. Brant, cold and exhausted, fingers and ears numb, was nonetheless mindful of the presence of the mammal on whose back he rode. He was in partnership with a creature of nature he had long admired. The Milky Way appeared as if someone had painted the sky with a large brush. Brant rode the whale in a trance-like state of mind throughout the night. Boy stopped periodically to rest along the way. During these stops the whales sang songs as if they were sitting around a campfire. They slept conscious of their need to stay above water, with one half of their brain operating while the other rested.

Brant's thirst was worsening. At least his hands were not as cold, clasped together around the fin as they were. By early morning, there were some distant clouds that looked like they might contain rain. He wondered if his booties could serve as a container to hold rainwater that he could drink the next day. To see if they leaked saltwater, he released his locked hands, held on to the fin with his right hand, and reached back to tug on his bootie to take it off and experiment. As soon as he let go, however, he fell off. Boy returned to investigate, his sensitive skin immediately telling him he had lost his passenger.

"Boy, I'm dying of thirst. I need water and you can't help me." Brant realized that he was talking to the whale with the expectation he would understand.

Boy lifted Brant on his head, turned, and slowly continued heading southwest.

Without the fin, Brant was holding on to barnacles again. One felt loose and something told Brant to pull it off. He did, and while carefully pressing his legs and other arm into the whale so he didn't fall, he placed the bottom of the barnacle to his lips and sucked. Instantly he tasted a slightly sweet, saltless liquid that barely coated his tongue. Several other barnacles surrounded him. Risking falling each time, he pried off one after another. It was difficult work for his numb fingers but soon all those within reach were gone, leaving white circular scars where they had been. His fingers were sore and bloody for the effort and within minutes his thirst returned. Even worse was that he had removed his handholds. Now, to stay on the whale he had to use even more muscle power, stretching his arms out and pressing them against the whale's back. Exhausted, he finally let go, staying on the whale's back without holding on for about five seconds before a wave washed him overboard.

Boy stopped as usual, dove and surfaced alongside Brant. He dove again and came up in the so-called "spy-hop" position, looking back to the northeast. Brant followed his gaze and saw several orcas 50 yards away. He looked again and saw that one of them had a large, bright orange object in front of it. Brant saw that he was pushing a rubber raft. Soon the orcas were surrounding Brant, making whistling noises and acting like children who had a wonderful present to offer a friend. The orca that brought it to him danced in the water and nodded its head several times. Then it turned and dove, followed by the others, surfacing to breathe 100 yards back to the northeast.

The raft, a four-person Avon, was about nine-feet long. Along the top of the starboard tube someone with good penmanship had written "Bella Bella" with a black magic marker. It must have detached from the boat Brant saw go down. The images of the previous night flooded back into his memory. He wondered if the crew had been rescued and hoped that the very harnesses that kept them from being washed overboard had not brought them down with the boat.

On the other side of the raft the large adult male

whale was nodding its head up and down as if telling Brant the raft was intended for him. Brant did not hesitate. Within a few minutes he was taking stock of the supplies. Halfway through he realized the whales were gone. Relieved, he continued taking inventory more intensely. Now it was up to him alone to survive. He was only a two-day paddle from home. He believed with water and food he could survive. What a story he would have to tell! He started over, placing each object in the center of the raft before returning it to its proper place. The waves were relatively gentle, making the work easier.

By the time he finished he had located two small oars and a 9 square-foot triangular sail with sewn pockets for the oar handles. It could double for a shade and a rain catcher. The four items Brant considered to be the most vital included six quart containers of water, several boxes of nutrition bars, a box of motion sickness tablets and a Search and Rescue Transponder. He also found a short fillet knife, a signaling mirror, a first aid kit, a red box containing a flare gun with five flare cartridges and two red parachute flares, a sea anchor, a 75-foot line, some nylon string and a box of plastic bags.

Although he was thirsty, he knew he had to conserve water. He carefully opened one of the jars and took a few sips, licking his dry lips. The whales were nowhere in sight. He wondered if this time they had left him for good. He reflected on the intelligence and generosity the orca displayed in bringing the raft back to the man.

Brant needed energy so he unwrapped one of the nutrition bars and bit off a small section before carefully placing it back in the box. Next, before checking the wind and seeing what must be done to set sail for home, he studied the electronic device labeled SART. He had never seen one before, let alone used one. It was high visibility orange thermoplastic with stainless steel screws sealed with O-rings. A security label over a push button switch read, "This SART is an emergency device for use only in grave and imminent danger." Brant was elated. No doubt he qualified. Thinking the unit would send a signal to the search and rescuers that were undoubtedly looking for him, he pulled off the label and pressed the button. Brant knew he had traveled well over 100 miles across the Pacific. He did not know, however, that the SART would only work if a searching ship with radar was within five or six miles and then only if the unit was held one meter above sea level. He also didn't know that an aircraft searching for him would have to be within 30 miles. Worse, he did not know that the lithium battery, though having a life span of 5 years, would only allow him to transmit for 8 hours or, if on standby, for 96 hours.

Brant unwittingly set the handheld SART in the transpond mode on the raft floor and began rigging a sail. He placed the handles of the small oars into the pockets of the sail. He then did his best to head toward where he thought the sun rose hours before. Brant owned a small sailboat, a 19-foot Maine Lobster Boat. He was not a great sailor by any means but he did know enough about sailing to manage the raft.

The prevailing wind was blowing directly from the northeast, driven by the summer north Pacific High, which rotates clockwise. It sent strong breezes from east to west in mid latitudes, switching to northwest as you sail north (off British Columbia the northwest trades would be prevailing). He knew he'd have to tack but his jury-rigged sailing raft was not efficient enough to make any headway. Without an oar in the water to use as a rudder he couldn't even sail on a beam reach. The winds, blowing smoothly at around 12 knots, turned him in the opposite direction. He let the wind turn the raft around to see if it could sail downwind. He sailed back toward Hawaii for a few minutes. Then he stopped, took the sail off and placed it over his head for sun protection. Brant mounted the oars in their brackets and turned around again. After an hour it seemed he hadn't made any progress. He drank more water than he should have. He fell back, exhausted and cursed loudly. Just before he fell asleep, he heard whales blowing.

Last Song of the Whales

8. The Choice

Brant fell back in the raft after his exhausting effort to paddle into the wind. He was unable to move, even to see if the whales he heard blow were "his" whales. Instead he just lay there, too tired to sleep and too weak to move. That is until he felt the entire raft being lifted up on the back of one of the leviathans. Afraid to move lest he upset the precarious balance and frozen in his first relatively comfortable position since first jumping on the whale, Brant stayed where he had collapsed. The sun was high overhead. He waited by the minute for the raft to fall back into the ocean but it didn't.

Brant remembered reading about how humpback mothers would occasionally give their young calves a ride when making their first ocean crossing together. Nonetheless, it did not seem possible that the successful balancing could continue. Sure enough it wasn't long before the raft was floating on the water again. There was no sudden drop, just the feeling of the whale's back bumping up against the bottom as he moved from underneath. Brant's strength was returning and he was glad he was back in the water. The whales had taken him farther from his destination. In spite of his recent failure, however, he grabbed the oars, one of which had nearly fallen out of its bracket, and continued paddling back against the wind.

The whales surrounded him, even the mother and her calf. Boy came close, maybe three yards away, and rolled on his back. Exposing his white belly, he turned slightly and waved one of his large fins. Brant was amazed at this huge creature's agility, due in large part to its flippers. Brant thought the gesture had meaning, although he didn't know what. Boy rolled back over and looked at him. At that moment Brant understood that he was about to make an important choice. His options were to continue trying to paddle against the wind only a few days away from Salmon Beach; to sit and wait for a boat to come by; or to stay with the whales on what was obviously going to be nearly a month-long journey to the Hawaiian Islands, where he knew they wintered. Was he crazy? How could he even consider it? Or was staying with the whales really his best chance? He looked into the whales' eyes. The larger whale was moving off, slapping his tail, as if to tell Boy it was time to let the man go.

While Brant was deciding, he lifted the SART as high over his head as he could. He had one last chance before making his choice. He wished the box contained directions. He looked behind the unit in case he could learn something about its range. That's when he noticed he had left the SART on transponder mode. He worried that doing so drained the batteries significantly. He quickly switched it to standby, thinking this meant that if a ship with radar got within range the machine would somehow notify him. He hoped he hadn't wasted too much of the batteries' life. Regardless, his chances of encountering a boat would be just as good whichever direction he went.

"OK, Boy. I'm going with you. I think I can sail the direction you all are going."

He mounted the oars into the sail again. He wanted to see just how well the boat could sail downwind without a rudder and with the current brisk breeze. He could change his mind if it didn't work. Brant balanced the blades on his thighs and leaned back against the cross pontoon to get out of the way. The boat immediately lurched forward, soon gaining a speed of around three knots. Brant remembered using Gilles' GPS when sailing his own boat and estimated that he was going about half as fast. Under similar conditions his boat cruised at around five or six knots. That was what the whales seemed to be averaging. What the hell? If he was going to die he may as well do so while on the adventure of a lifetime. The whales apparently were satisfied with Brant's decision, except for the large one, Brant thought. They started clucking and whistling while they swam playfully alongside the raft.

Brant was on his way to Hawaii. Or so he thought.

9. The Survivor

Angela left the library and returned to the Coast Guard office. The office crew informed her that the second day's search resumed at noon as she was told it would. There was nothing for her to do but check back throughout the day so she returned to the library. She Googled everything she could find about humpback whales. She still was trying to determine if it was possible for one to do what she saw with her own eyes.

She was especially interested in a 2006 article entitled, "The Structure of the Cerebral Cortex of the Humpback Whale—Megaptera novaeangliae (Cetacea, Mysticeti, Balaenopteridae)," by Patrick R. Hof and Estel Van der Gucht. It was published in *The Anatomical Record*, the official journal of the American Association of Anatomists. The article explained that a humpback whale's brain, similar in complexity to that of a dolphin's, contains a certain neuron cell and spindle cells also found in humans. The authors suggested this was evidence that the humpback evolved alongside the hominids. They claimed the biology of the humpback whale was not well understood. No studies have been conducted on its brain composition that might explain its extensive behavioral and social abilities. The authors concluded that more attention should be paid to the "intricate communication skills, coalition formation, cooperation, cultural transmission and tool usage" of humpbacks, especially because it is likely that some of these abilities are related to comparable complexities in human brains.

The article led Angela to start searching "whale intelligence." She immediately found numerous sites about a scientist named John Lilly, who died in 2001 in his Maui home. She was amazed by his work, as controversial as it seemed to be. A physician, scientist and psychologist, Lilly was a pioneer in the study of interspecies communication between humans and dolphins. While researching the physical structures of the brain and consciousness at the University of Pennsylvania, he wrote an article that envisioned a time when killing whales and dolphins would cease "not from a law being passed but from each human understanding innately that these are ancient, sentient earth residents, with tremendous intelligence and enormous life force. Not something to kill but someone to learn from."

Angela considered all of this. If the whale was not just some wild ocean creature and truly possessed the kind of consciousness that so many people, including these scientists, believed they did, why would it want to hurt her husband? Perhaps it had been a killer whale that mistook Brant for a seal. But then orca attacks on humans were extremely rare according to everything she was reading. Maybe she was right after all about her husband being in the care of a humpback whale. And what if the whale had some reason for taking him?

About an hour before the sun started setting, she made one last trip to the Coast Guard. Each time she walked in the door her heart was in her throat as she anticipated the news.

The man with the bandaged finger stood to greet her.

"Ma'am, our planes just landed. I'm sorry. We didn't find him. We're going to try again tomorrow. We'll extend the search further out to sea and in the direction the prevailing winds might have blown him."

Angela lowered her head and nodded.

"We do have more news. Remember the boat that was reported missing?"

She looked up, not knowing what to expect.

"While we think the boat sunk we did find one of the individuals who was on board. According to his wife there were two people with her husband. We haven't located them either. The man we found is in a coma and not expected to live. He is in a Port Angeles hospital. I'm sorry to have to tell you this but…"

Angela thought she knew what he was going to say and interrupted him.

"Can you tell me what he was wearing? Did he have a life jacket on?"

"Yes, ma'am. He was wearing a life jacket under a large poncho-type rubber raincoat."

"Was he wearing a wet or dry suit?"

Now the man understood the point she was making. "No, ma'am. If he had, he might not be in such bad shape."

"Anything else you can tell me?"

"No, ma'am. We really can't tell you much more. We're not allowed to disclose the victim's name. The captain did want me to ask you a question. Was your husband carrying any kind of emergency light?"

Angela shook her head. "Why do you ask?"

"If he was, we would go out again tonight when it's clear. Searching for a light in a dark ocean would be better than searching for a man in the daylight. We thought of it because the man was found gripping a flashlight. It wasn't working but he still was holding on to it."

Last Song of the Whales

10. The Tow

The perils of being in a raft 200 miles southwest of Canada were logically not as dire as the risks of crossing the Pacific Ocean in it. Nonetheless Brant was content with his decision. Maybe the idea of dying alone so close to home was more unbearable than being in the company of the whales and meeting some unforeseen calamity. In any event, if there was any chance he might survive the voyage the experience would be worth whatever risks he faced.

Sailing was not easy. To follow the whales he had to steer the raft without a rudder by adjusting the sail's angle to the wind. The physical strength needed to hold the sail in a stiff breeze was already straining all the muscles in his back, arms and shoulders. The pain in his injured shoulder was most severe when the wind blew hard, forcing him to rest every 20 to 30 minutes. He'd put down the sail, stretch a little, then eat and drink some of his rations. When he stopped to do this, the whales would continue onward except for Boy, who would float 50 to 100 yards away and wait. Sometimes he would nudge the raft forward.

Once in a while, the whales let him sail past them. This happened one time when they were involved with some project, although Brant hardly could imagine what it was. Brant stopped, watched and listened, eventually concluding that they were learning a new song. When the one learning would make an obvious mistake they would stop. The apparent teacher—and they all took turns, including the calf—would repeat a phrase and the whale having difficulty would repeat it. It reminded Brant of how he learned new songs on his guitar.

Usually Brant would just continue sailing past the singing whales. If he was on the right trajectory, the whales simply caught up and traveled with him. If he was off course, the whales would call to him and he would have to dismantle the sail and paddle around until he could sail in the right direction again.

Brant was starting to recognize the whales' different personalities. For example, he considered the calf to be rebellious. This was based on it always being in trouble with its mother. This usually happened right after the mother, who seemed shy, was reprimanded by the larger humpback when she paid too much attention to Brant. The mother seemed to like it when the calf was near the man but her escort seemed to think otherwise.

Brant was drinking water when Boy came back after the whales got too far in front. The calf was with him. Boy and the calf would swim circles around the raft until Brant thought it would tip over from the wake. Soon the mother and the large humpback appeared. The male came up from behind the mother at high speed, bumping her with his own body. At first Brant thought it was a sexual act. After seeing this happen again at different times, he was convinced the male was merely asserting his strong declaration about keeping the calf away from the human. The mother, apparently in response, chirped and whistled at the calf in a manner Brant thought caused the calf to reluctantly stop playing around the raft and return to its mother's side. The smaller adult male seemed to mind its own business. He showed little interest in Brant and although he was a good singer, he did not play as physically as the others.

Night arrived quickly and with it a heavy rain and howling winds. It was cold and in spite of the dry suit, Brant's body heat was escaping through his head. His will to survive, however, was improving. He was no longer just reacting and felt there was a new level of mindfulness in his every action. He had emptied one of the quart bottles and now took a big drink from a full one. Then he laid the sail down to collect rain water. After filling the jugs, he stowed them away and reset the sailing rig.

The wind increased until it was blowing roughly 15 to 20 knots. It took all of Brant's strength to sail. The waves increased and he found himself surfing down the back of them. He knew that any one of them might flip him over. After a while he could not hold on to the sail or control the raft well enough to avoid capsizing. He attached the oars and tucked the sail away, almost being broached in the process. He rowed as fast as he could, trying to keep the raft aligned with the waves. He surfed down the face of one and up the back of another.

The squall came and left. The wind died down and a light rain replaced the more violent precipitation. There wasn't enough wind to sail and Brant couldn't row anymore. He covered his head with the sail and tried to rest. Several hours later he woke to silence. The rain had stopped and the sky was clear, displaying the blackest sky and the brightest stars Brant ever saw. He ate an entire nutrition bar and took several gulps of water.

Brant had not seen or heard any sign of the whales for hours. A subtle swath of silvery reflection to the east began to obscure the bright stars. The sun would rise in another hour. Brant was alone and now further from home. He had used up more energy and food than if he just waited back where he received the raft. Why did he make the foolish choice to head southwest with the whales?

By the time the sun was well above the eastern horizon there wasn't enough wind to set sail and Brant was still too tired to row. Although the waves pitched and turned his raft, it seemed stable enough and he did not worry about capsizing. It had been at least three hours since he last saw the whales. He cursed out loud, angry with his arrogant assumption that he was somehow important to them. This emotion vanished, however, when he saw a spout half a mile off. Within minutes Boy was rolling on his back next to the raft and showing his great fins. Brant looked to see if the other whales were around but saw no sign of them. Boy obviously could not understand why Brant wasn't following him. He swam off, stopped, looked back and then returned to the raft several times. Obviously Brant would not be able to keep up with the whales by sailing and rowing if the winds were going to be as undependable as this morning. As for rowing, Brant knew it would take far too much energy for him to survive.

There had to be another way besides riding the whale or being carried in its jaws. He noticed the line in the raft just as Boy's dorsal fin came close by it. Maybe, just maybe, it would work. Brant grabbed the line and jumped overboard, swimming onto Boy's back. He tied a loop in the end of the line and started to place it over the fin, thinking it would be easier to slip it on and off. He quickly realized, however, that it would likely float off once the dorsal fin submerged. On the other hand, if he tied it at the base and Boy dove down he could pull the raft headfirst underwater. He remembered the knife. He could always cut the line if that happened. He tied the line to the fin, swam back to the raft and attached it to the stainless steel ring on the front of the raft with an easy to release bowline knot. He climbed back in the raft, stuck the knife sheath and knife in the belt of his kayak life vest and held on.

"Let's go, Boy!" He called out like a dog musher. Unbelievably, Boy wasted no time. He began pulling and swimming as close to the surface as he could. The raft lunged each time his tail propelled him forward with its powerful upstroke and then dipped slightly on the down stroke as the dorsal fin submerged. It was not the best towing arrangement for a voyage across the Pacific Ocean to Hawaii but it was working.

Last Song of the Whales

11. The Possibilities

When Loni checked her e-mail, she was curious to see if there was a reply from the woman who claimed her husband was taken by a humpback. She was not sure why she was so interested in this case. The whole affair was preposterous. Although she had sympathy for the woman's story, she almost wished she had not volunteered to help. She could hear her colleagues now. "So, crazy Loni thinks a humpback whale swallowed a professor in British Columbia and might be taking him on a free trip in its belly to Hawaii." Oh well, she thought, she really did not care all that much about what her colleagues might say.

Loni studied the photos Angela sent. One revealed just how close to the boat the whale had come. The whale couldn't have been more than three or four feet away. The beads of water and spray in the image made the whale look like it had fur. Other photos showed the notched dorsal fin. Loni scanned through the dozen images looking for one that showed the flukes' underside. If she had one, she could have her staff look through nearly 400 of their own identified whales. She also could call Cascadia Research, headed by her friend and well-known researcher, John Calambokidis. It was his research that concluded that the humpback population went from nearly 300,000 whales to a low of 1,500 before whaling was banned worldwide. It climbed back to around 20,000 in 2010. He and his colleagues were preparing a public online catalog of more than 3,500 fluke identification photos of humpbacks in the Pacific. This would give them a one in nine chance of identifying the whale, for whatever good it would do. There were no photos of flukes, however. Loni was relieved. She considered all the extra work it would have required to try and match photos and all for what she thought was a wild goose chase.

Loni left a message with her assistant, Akamu, asking him to see what information was available about the Vancouver whales that might have some bearing on this matter. Angela's question, Loni thought, was fair enough.

If the whale was one of those that stayed year-round in British Columbia then the search for it would be a vastly different affair than if it migrated to Hawaii. Loni told Akamu to let her know when the tagged whale started its migration from B.C. to Hawaii.

Loni was 10 minutes late for her graduate class. The university's official policy allowed the class to dismiss itself if the instructor was not there 10 minutes after class started. This group of students never would have considered it. This was not only their favorite class but Loni was often 5 or 10 minutes late. They just began without her. Today, when Loni arrived, a bright young man named Rupert Vanderhoven was arguing with an equally sharp student named Leslie Stephenson.

Apparently Leslie had been blaming global warming for the increasing number of whales and dolphins dying around the world from ingesting saxitoxin. Saxitoxin was a poison that cyanobacteria, a type of blue-green algae, produced.

Leslie sounded more emotional than usual.

"Have you ever seen what happens to a dolphin that ingests this crap that is invading our oceans? First they start swimming in a twisting, corkscrew manner. They defecate and regurgitate and have convulsions. Next paralysis sets in and just prior to death they go into respiratory failure. This process can take several days to a week. When are people going to wake up? How can you, someone about to earn a doctorate in marine biology, feed me the same crap George Bush's crew fed the world for eight years about global warming?"

As usual Rupert kept his cool. He knew that Leslie actually liked him, certainly more than most of the rest of the class did.

"Look, Leslie, red tides have been around for a long time. Deaths from it were reported in Cuba and Australia in the early 1800s. Just because someone has changed the name "red tide" to "harmful algal blooms" doesn't change why nature produces this phenomenon. It doesn't make things better or worse. It is a natural cycle. To blame HABs on global warming is simply not good science. Global warming has become a boogieman like communism. It gets blamed for everything. HABs don't have anything to do with global warming and everything to do with phosphorous and nitrogen from agricultural runoff. Period."

John Griffen, an African-American student from

Honolulu, jumped in, apparently taking Rupert's side, something he rarely did.

"Rupert has a point. I would add that the reason we are hearing so much about algal blooms and the apparent increase in frequency and severity of them in various parts of the world is more related to increased observation efforts and advances in species identification methods than in some new problem."

Rupert was bolstered by this unexpected support.

"John's right on. It is the same with all this global warming doom and gloom. Things are happening, sure, but nature, not humans, is responsible for whatever changes we are seeing in the world. Global warming hasn't caused any real problems. The only thing causing problems is people believing it is a threat."

Loni politely interjected. "I think this is a great conversation but for now let's stay with our assigned topic relating to marine algae. Now who can tell me what is the main cause of cyanobacteria growth?"

One student yelled out, "Nutrient runoffs from agriculture, like Rupert said."

"That's correct," said Loni.

Rupert was on a roll and jumped in again.

"Conclusion? Phosphates and nitrogen are causing HABs, not global warming and it always..."

Loni interrupted. "And what increases phosphates and nitrogen in ocean waters besides agricultural runoff?" She looked at the class to make sure Rupert would not dominate the conversation.

No one answered so she answered her own question. "Decaying organic matter."

She continued. "Do you remember last week when I quoted some stats about dead zones from the World Resources Institute?"

"Yeah," one of the students confidently answered. "It said dead zones are a rapidly growing environmental crises and that more than 400 have been identified worldwide. The one in the Gulf of Mexico near the mouth of the Mississippi River has grown to around 7,500 square miles and is still growing."

"So what do dead zones have to do with decaying organic matter and toxic algal blooms?" Loni asked.

Jessie saw where she was going. "These dead zones are hypoxic or lacking oxygen. Some are anoxic, meaning they virtually have no oxygen at all. Although Rupert is right that one reason for this is the excessive nitrogen and phosphorus caused by runoff and pollution, like what's happening where the Mississippi runs into the Gulf, there are other important reasons. Dead fish, animals and plants, including phytoplankton, also produce too much nitrogen, causing hypoxic conditions."

Loni continued. "Yes, so this influx of nitrogen leads to eutrophication, which is a fancy word for excessive plant growth caused by too many nutrients. This, in turn, promotes toxic and non-toxic algal blooms. The decaying biomass of the bacterial decomposition of the blooms depletes oxygen. Creatures in the system are hurt both by eating the toxins and starving for oxygen.

"Stay with me. I'm going to get to the global warming factor. Seasonal upwellings and winds cause such nutrient-rich deposits in deep water to mix with surface waters. This fertilization of the upper layers of water and the sun causes the phytoplankton to grow too fast and the cycle begins. When ocean temperatures rise this cycle overcomes cyanobacterial's ability to produce oxygen normally. Remember most of our atmospheric oxygen comes from ocean photosynthesis, not from land vegetation exchanges between oxygen and carbon dioxide. All this will be on the test so if you don't understand it now is the time to ask."

No one was willing to admit they didn't get it yet but most did not.

"An additional factor," Loni continued, "that will not be on the test but you should know about, is that oxygen's solubility also is reduced when temperatures are higher."

Loni looked at Leslie, who was smiling a sinister smile. Leslie chimed in.

"So global warming IS combining with ocean pollution, such as that created by shrimp farms, animal manure, fertilizers and decaying biomass, which are both natural and unnatural. This results in an unprecedented overstimulation of algal blooms and is destroying our oceans. Moreover, this whole issue has remained largely under the radar because, unlike large catastrophic events, this type of pollution has been occurring at a low enough level over a long enough period of time to avoid attention. If there is a major increase in any of these factors the air you and I breathe could be affected. Yeah, Rupert. Let's ignore global warming."

Loni spoke again, partly to avoid an argument between Leslie and Rupert.

"I don't know if you can say it is unprecedented, Leslie. Many scientists believe that the last great mass extinction, 65 million years ago, was directly caused by the cycle of algal blooms and the anoxia you describe. I think we are a long way from that. It is true that we haven't seen so many dead zones and such a proliferation of HABs in recorded history. Global warming and pollution seem to be causing a massive competition between different varieties of algae, each trying to create a more toxic chemical with which to kill the other. This is a serious problem for us in two ways. First, we are at risk when we eat shellfish but more and more we are at risk from eating too much fish of any kind or even when swimming in areas with HABs.

"The second way, as I said earlier, is that it could put all of life on earth at risk. It could be curtains for all of us if some catastrophic event causes even larger percentages of the ocean to go anoxic. Remember the phytoplankton provides up to 70 percent of earth's oxygen and we already have more then 400 dead zones worldwide. In 2006, along the coast of Oregon, some of my colleagues recorded the most long-lasting hypoxia on record. It was the first time we've seen zero levels of oxygen in that area."

Loni realized she was probably going too far with this. It really was not her style to be so gloomy. Still she did want to add another piece to the puzzle before the class ended.

"There is one other important factor that unfortunately is largely under the radar. You all know about the immense plastic garbage patches that accumulate in the five oceanic gyres around the world. The worst is perhaps between here and Canada and now may be at least three times the size of Texas. Last month we talked about how mammals and birds are dying from ingesting the plastic and the poisoned chemicals that plastic absorbs. More of the plastic story directly relates to our discussion. A major scientific study by Maso *et al* identified the presence of alien marine species that are thriving on the plastic debris. Such species include barnacles, polychaete worms, bryozoans, hydroids, mollusks, sea grasses and seeds. What is significant is that researchers only found these organisms thriving where there were large toxic algal blooms! No one understands why yet."

The students were looking at their watches so Loni

knew class was about over.

"Your assignment for next week is to list three routes by which atmospheric nitrogen is converted into nutrient nitrogen in today's world. Then answer these questions. How many millions of tons of nitrogen are 'fixed' by each route in a year? What are the 'fixation' trends and what does this imply for the state of natural and human managed ecosystems? The assignment will be on the forum so you don't have to write it down."

Luana Malo raised her hand and began talking while everyone was packing up. She was one of the few native Hawaiian students in Loni's class. She always spoke so that the class had to strain to hear her.

"Dr. Stern, earlier you said a major event could trigger a catastrophe relating to our ability to breathe oxygen. Yesterday in my economics class we learned that global consumption of meat is expected to increase by more than 50 percent within the next 25 years. Even in the U.S. manure from animals does not legally have to be treated like human sewage. Could this be a big enough event?"

Loni shrugged her shoulders. "I doubt it but it certainly would contribute to the problem. Also, and this relates to global warming again," she smiled at Rupert, who was looking a little sheepish but planning a rebuttal at the same time, "as organic chemical runoff relating to meat consumption continues to increase hypoxic areas in our oceans, the bacteria from the decaying organic matter leads to an increase in the release of nitrous oxide. This also is known as laughing gas, which is a potent greenhouse gas."

Class was over. As the students were walking out the door, Sonny Frey, always good for a joke, offered the last words. "This is great. Cyanobacteria, let's just call it algae, comes on the scene to produce oxygen in the first place to allow for life on this planet. Now it is on the verge of killing us. The only good news I'm leaving with today is that when we go we'll be laughing from the nitrous oxide!"

12. The Ghost Net

As the whale pulled the raft forward, Brant was amazed at how he swam higher in the water than when he was swimming free. He used his great flippers like wings. Each one was at least 10 or 11-feet long with a rounded leading edge and a thin trailing edge like an airplane wing. Large bumps jutting out from the leading edge gave it a serrated look. Using them in ways Brant had not previously observed, the whale maintained a gliding undulation along the surface to keep the raft from lurching forward after each upstroke of its mighty tail flukes. What impressed him the most, however, was how Boy was so perfectly engaged in the business of towing the raft. How he understood to do something like this, something he never experienced before, was beyond Brant's comprehension.

"Boy, you really are amazing." Brant found himself

talking to the whale more and more. He was now convinced that Boy somehow understood what he was saying. In fact, he was a little sorry he named the whale "Boy" as it seemed demeaning to him now. Perhaps, he thought, "Professor" would have been more appropriate. Brant did not really even know if it was a male. In any case, his respect for Boy was real and he felt Boy recognized it.

Boy pulled the raft this way for several days and nights. Brant kept his knife ready to cut the line in case Boy forgot what he was doing and dove. They had caught up with the other whales the first day. Every five or six hours, they would stop to rest. During these times Brant would sleep soundly, not having to concentrate on the line.

One morning, 12 or more bottlenose dolphins joined the pod. They swam and did flips around the raft and looked at Brant with amusement. Although Boy remained on course, the other whales were doing various maneuvers with the dolphins as if playing "follow the leader." It seemed like they were communicating with one another. Brant never imagined that whales and dolphins enjoyed such a relationship.

On his third or fourth day at sea, Brant couldn't remember which, a large black cloud moved overhead and gently poured out its contents. Boy stopped and as the raft bumped against him, he lifted his head and opened his mouth up wide. During all his whale watching in Barkley Sound, Brant never saw anything like it. Boy was drinking rainwater! Why not? Although 50 million years of evolution obviously had designed ways for the whale to ingest sufficient fresh water from his food sources, a fresh drink must be a special thing.

The rain stopped and the cloud moved in a southerly direction as the evening sun began to depart from the red and purple sky it had painted. The contrast between the sunset colors and the disappearing rain cloud was striking. Leaving its usual gift of negative ions, the falling water had split countless neutral air particles, freeing electrons to charge billions more. This deeply revitalized Brant, a stark contrast to the discomforts the rain previously offered him. He felt like he was regaining a long lost balance. It was as if his brainwaves were being supercharged, fine-tuning the synchronization of his hemispheres. He looked at Boy and imagined that the whale was experiencing the same thing.

Boy resumed swimming. The other whales also had stopped to enjoy the rain, although they didn't seem to be drinking it in as Boy had. Brant and Boy were now back on course but the others remained involved with teaching the calf some lesson. Brant knew they would catch up soon enough. Meanwhile, after drinking the remaining rainwater from the bottom of the raft, Brant was teaching himself one of the songs the whales sang the night before. It had a melody that he was able to capture in his mind but he still couldn't hum it. He thought it would be easier to replicate it by whistling but his lips were too parched. At least his head wasn't being burnt by the sun any longer since he could not use the sail for shade.

Within 15 minutes Brant heard the other whales blowing. They were about 100 yards behind him. Then Boy let out a grunt such as Brant had never heard, stopped his forward momentum and made a failed attempt at a sharp left turn. His entire head was entangled in a huge gill net that pulled him back when his right flipper also became caught. Feeling trapped and struggling to keep his blowholes above water Boy tried to escape by diving. Brant felt the raft's bow quickly dip down and he managed to cut the line just in time. Boy's powerful dive was not enough to free him and may have worsened his entrapment in the net. A large portion of the lines holding the netting were wrapped about his tail flukes. The lines holding up the net stretched to the north and south as far as Brant could see. Boy now realized his situation and knew any movement could make things worse. He stopped struggling and let out a sigh that chilled Brant to the bone.

Remaining still, however, presented another problem. The weight of the many gill nets tangled up together was pulling Boy down. This required him to carefully use his flippers and flukes to keep his blowhole above water. Brant realized his predicament and jumped off the raft with his knife, careful not to get wrapped in the nylon lines. He saw different colored nets with different sizes of netting. These were the infamous "ghost nets" he read about. "Ghost nets" was the term being used for the discarded or dislodged drift nets that eventually merged together into one large mass and drifted dangerously across the oceans, waiting for prey. They were responsible for killing more whales than whaling or the toxic pollution that saturates whale blubber and whale mother's milk. Just last week, although it seemed a lifetime ago, Brant had read a report from the International Whaling Commission that said over 300,000 cetaceans die annually because of the kind of entanglements he was now witnessing.

Boy looked Brant in the eye as Brant approached from the whale's left. The look conveyed a mutual trust and recognition of the seriousness of the situation. The other whales heard Boy's cry, which apparently served as a warning. They all kept their distance from the netting and seemed to know exactly what was happening. They watched the man intently. Brant felt their gaze and the heightened sense of responsibility it gave him.

He carefully started cutting the lines away from Boy, working his way to the tail. He wanted to free it first so Boy could better use it to stay above water. Brant's heart stopped each time he felt the netting grab at him. Even with the buoyancy his dry suit and life vest provided he had to be careful not to get in trouble himself. He moved gently and cautiously. He flattened himself out on the surface and floated over the wall of death.

Just as he was about to reach a place on Boy's tail where he could cut the line and net, the netting underneath Brant suddenly jerked him to his left. It grabbed his foot and was pulling him down. Brant's growing sense of inner balance prevented him from panicking. He did not resist or struggle. Instead, he carefully twisted his foot up and away from the lines and regained his floating posture. That's when he saw why the net moved. Just below him, a shark, maybe 12-foot long with jaws agape and also trapped in the net, was trying to bite him. It lashed out at him again and again, gathering more and more netting into its mouth and around its teeth each time. Carefully, several feet from the sharp teeth, Brant backstroked over the netting until his head touched Boy and he was out of the range of the shark's jaws.

Brant talked to the whale encouragingly and began cutting the line. He also thought about the shark's plight and felt a deep sense of empathy. He knew these great and ancient creatures, here before the dinosaurs, were on the verge of extinction. Unlike the whales, sharks had few advocates. As a professor of environmental science, Brant knew the sharks played an important role in maintaining the balance of healthy plankton by eating those that fed upon it. Without the sharks, the plankton would be over-consumed. Considering that ocean plankton provided most of earth's oxygen, this would have grave consequences.

Brant was having no trouble cutting the lines and netting. Boy remained still, knowing that Brant was trying to help him. Unfortunately one line was embedded in a section of Boy's tail. If the epidermis closed over the line it could cause a debilitating infection. Brant removed it carefully. When he had finally managed to cut the netting away from the flukes, he swam gently along Boy's back cutting the netting as he went. It pulled away instantly except where it was attached to the dorsal fin. Careful to avoid cutting the towing line that was tied to the fin, Brant removed the remaining netting and it fell back into the sea. As it did, it added weight to the netting still attached to Boy's fin. It pulled him down so his blowholes were under water. Brant knew he had to move fast. He figured the whale only had another 20 minutes or so to survive before it drowned. He held his breath and dove to the tip of the flipper and began cutting again. After 10 dives, each one more demanding, his face, head and hands became numb and his eyes were burning from the cold saltwater. He finally managed to clear the net off the right flipper. Boy then used it and his tail to carefully right himself.

Brant moved to the left flipper next. Miraculously, it only had one 3/8 inch steel line draped over it with no netting. He tried cutting the rusted metal line with his knife but couldn't get through it. Careful to keep it from catching on the flipper's tubelike bumps, he used all his strength to pull the line over the tip of the flipper. He was constantly at risk of getting his feet caught in the net below. All that was left now was the portion of the netting that held Boy's mouth down. Brant swam to it and cut it as he had done along the back but it did not fall away. Upon closer examination he saw a portion of the line was wedged between the whale's lips and the baleen plates. Brant held the line with both hands. With his feet placed against Boy, he pulled as hard as he could until the line dropped out of the way, pulling the rest of the net with it. Although he was free, Boy was still surrounded by the plastic death trap. He knew he couldn't go forward, to the right or to the left without getting tangled again. Although humpbacks can turn on a dime and often back up enough to slam a rival male, their backing prowess is limited. Boy seemed to understand his predicament and remained still.

Brant was exhausted. Careful to avoid the shark, which no longer was thrashing and appeared to be dying, he swam back to the boat, pulling the towing line with him. He tied it to the raft again and then barely managed to climb aboard. After several minutes of needed rest, he ate a nutrition bar and drank some water. He attached the oars and with all his might paddled to pull the whale straight back. He cried out in pain with each stroke until he realized he was pulling Boy out. Once Boy started moving he helped with his own backward motion, making it easier for Brant. When Boy was clear of the netting, the mother whale and the large male moved alongside him to be sure he was safe. Knowing that Boy was exhausted, the whales located themselves a safe distance from the wall of netting and rested. When Brant's adrenalin level subsided he fell to the bottom of the raft, unconscious.

13. The Tag

Although the Coast Guard officially called off the search for her husband, Angela went out on the ocean from Ucluelet Harbor whenever the weather allowed. She went with whomever she could pay to take her to search for the humpback whale with the notched fin. After several days she realized it was useless. The winter weather had set in, making it almost impossible to be on the water. She made one last stop at the library and read her e-mails before heading for Victoria and the ferry to the U.S. Then she would go on to Seattle to catch her flight to Mexico. There was nothing more she could do from Salmon Beach. There was an e-mail from Loni Stern telling her they couldn't find any images of notches in the dorsal fins as she had described. They did, however, see a number with chunks missing from various other places. There was no way to determine if the whale involved with her husband was a resident B.C. whale. She was sorry.

Angela read the note without emotion. She knew this likely would be the case. She was about to close her e-mail when she noticed a postscript after Loni's signature.

> PS By the way, we did note that we have a whale with a GPS tag on it from your neck of the woods. It left for its migration to Hawaii the day after your husband went missing. It was feeding off the coast of Vancouver Island about 60 miles north of Barkley Sound. I am telling you so you know it wouldn't have been too late in the season for your whale to be heading our way. I'm sorry we don't have better news.

Angela wrote back:

> Dear Dr. Stern,
> Thanks again. I don't have much hope anymore. Unless, miraculously, the whale still has him in its mouth, I suppose I will have to accept my husband's fate. I'm heading back to our home in Mexico."

Angela signed the letter, "Yours truly." She started to

send it when she, too, had an afterthought for her own postscript.

> PS Dr. Stern, you say a whale with a tag on it left the day after my husband was taken. If somehow my husband is still with the whale, might that whale and the one with the tag meet up along the way and travel together? And if so, would it be possible to keep me posted as to the tagged whale's location? Maybe I'll come visit you and watch him arrive.

Obviously Angela had not completely let go of the idea that the whale still had her husband. She did know, however, what an impossible idea it was. She was beginning to think Loni and the others were right. No one believed the whale took Brant in its mouth. She sent the e-mail anyway, stopped by the Coast Guard offices to say goodbye and headed toward the ferry.

Last Song of the Whales

14. The Bonding

When Brant came to, he couldn't sit up. Every muscle and joint had gone on strike. A portion of a nutrition bar and a jug of water were in reach but the muscles in his hands would not work to access them. He noticed the raft wasn't moving except for gently rocking in the waves. He remembered he was connected to Boy and assumed the whale was still resting.

Brant forced himself up on one elbow. He grabbed the water and drank it while looking for the whales. All five were surrounding the raft in a perfect circle with their massive heads facing it. The unique sight forced Brant to bolt upright in spite of his pain.

"What's going on, guys?" Then, looking at the calf's mother, Brant said, "Excuse me. I should have said guys and gal." He didn't know the sex of the 15-foot calf but he thought it also was a female.

The whales, as if synchronized, nodded their heads in unison. The calf ducked out of sight and within a minute breached 50 feet from the boat, splashing everyone as it landed. Boy looked at Brant like he wanted to join the calf. Brant untied the line from the raft and threw it over his back. Boy rolled over and clapped his great flippers as if applauding. The other two whales dove in opposite directions and then breached their bodies almost completely out of the water. Brant was overwhelmed by their grace and power.

The large male, whom Brant called Bluto, was still floating quietly. He looked at Brant as if to say, "I take back my negative feelings about that young whale you call Boy taking you with us. Thank you for what you did."

The evening light was fading when the whales joined Bluto again in their circle around the raft. Brant obviously was the center of attention and could only imagine it was because of his rescuing Boy. Suddenly Boy began singing a song unlike any Brant had heard him or the other whales sing before. It had a distinct melody, almost like a Lakota chant he knew, with repetitive short and long phrases. The sequence of phrases lasted for about five minutes before repeating themselves. Boy continued alone for 20 minutes, after which the other whales joined him.

"Son of a gun," Brant said out loud. "You guys are singing a 'thank you' song to me!"

Tears filled his eyes with an emotion that stemmed from some deep realization that the whales and he were as one, connected in unimaginable ways and far more similar than different. He thought about some of the books he read about whales and dolphins that claimed that whales were highly intelligent, spiritual beings. He remembered a particular scientific book by some psychologists. It was about a whale research project that studied the cognitive functioning of humpbacks in Stellwagen. One of the researchers, following in John Lilly's footsteps, concluded that the whale is another intelligent race that knows secret paths for living a balanced life. This researcher also wondered if whales migrated to areas with large human populations because of the bond that existed with humans and in the hope that humans eventually would realize it, too.

There was no doubt that Brant felt Boy's mystical energy the first time he appeared at Gilles' boat. Perhaps being overwhelmed at a psychic level caused Brant to step onto the whale. Now, however, he was more fully aware of how his energy and the whale's came from the same source. He remembered something he had read on a card about "whale medicine" and how the whale symbolized a time for remembering one's origins. He believed this is what he was learning to do.

Having spent so many years looking at the traditional ecological knowledge of Indigenous Peoples, Brant could not help but be aware of how they embraced a spiritual understanding about the sacredness of everything in nature. This awareness confirmed his earlier rejection of any organized religion in place of the agnostic idea that no one could know the details of something called "God." As he said the word to himself, he considered how often he used it in spite of his disbelief. He often said it during his time with the whales. He recalled exclaiming when he climbed aboard Boy for the first time, "My God. This is really happening."

He wondered *why* those were his first words. He was not a religious person. If he had believed in some all powerful savior or was arrogant enough to think he could beseech him or her or it with a personal request, would it not have been more reasonable if he had asked "God" for help rather than announce the obvious?

Brant believed in reason. He remembered a quote from Thomas Jefferson that he often shared with his students. "Question with boldness even the existence of a God because if there be one he must approve of the homage of reason more than that of blindfolded fears." Of course what would have been most reasonable was not to have mounted the whale in the first place. Once in danger, however, wouldn't it have been more accurate to say, "God, help me get through this. I must have been temporarily insane?"

Then again maybe he considered that his words were not for God at all but for himself or for the God he felt was part of him. Perhaps conversing with God was an expression of joy. He was known to invoke God's name during especially joyous moments. "God, this is wonderful!" is what he said upon seeing the Grand Canyon for the first time. He was sure he said "Oh, God" occasionally during intercourse. He also flattered several cooks with an appreciative, "God, this is delicious." If it had been an expression of joy it must have been the kind Ralph Waldo Emerson described when he wrote, "You shall have joy, or you shall have power, said God, you shall not have both."

Yes. The idea of joyfulness resonated in him even after the wondrous and horrifying events of the days and hours, even now when his fate was uncertain. He experienced an ecstasy that marks the pinnacle of living life and transcends everything one knows of life. How ironic that he was feeling so connected to life only now when faced with the probability of it ending. As he contemplated that, his heart absorbed every nuance, texture, feeling, thought, mystical impulse, universal vibration, intuitive wisdom, love and laughter the experience of joy can embody. Surely this was an example of how his Cherokee ancestors exercised their spiritual understandings.

When the whales finished the song, a good hour after Boy started it, they disbanded and headed out to sea. Boy circled around the raft waiting for Brant to connect it to the line. He knew just how far to swim so his dorsal fin was adjacent to the raft and within Brant's reach. While reconnecting the line the length of the young male's right side was less than 100 feet away, maneuvering into a shallow dive. As it did so Brant noticed a bright yellow plastic antenna sticking out of its side about 10 inches below the dorsal fin.

Last Song of the Whales

15. The Witness

Several days after arriving at her and Brant's casita in Mexico, Angela gathered friends and family to celebrate Brant's life and mourn his loss. She no longer had hope that he could be alive. Punta Fortuna, a small fishing village south of Manzanillo, offered her the tranquility she needed to make peace with what had happened. The local people were warm and friendly. They expressed their genuine grief and gave her their support.

To put closure on the ceremony, Angela invited several of Brant's friends to join her in their Temescal, the Aztec version of a traditional American Indian purification lodge. Brant had it built from a photograph he saw in a book. He, Angela and a number of friends sang and prayed together in it every Sunday night. Although he honored the Lakota tradition and relied upon it for his own spiritual path, sometimes he felt guilty that he knew so little about his own Cherokee culture.

After leaving the lodge Angela went inside to call Sue and Gilles. She wanted to share the day's events with them. They chose not to make the trip to Mexico from their home near Ontario. They knew Angela wouldn't mind. It was an expensive flight and they had said goodbye to Brant in their own way. As Angela picked up the phone she noticed two messages on her answering machine. She decided to check them after speaking with Sue.

"Angela, I'm so happy you called. We left several messages. We spoke with John Huffington's wife, Marlene, an hour ago. The man who was with John and his brother-in-law on the Bella Bella when it went down came out of his coma. He is going to be fine. His name is Danny Irving. I don't know much more about him."

"Thank God," Angela said.

"Angela." Sue paused and Angela knew she was going to say something equally important but more difficult.

"Angela, he saw Brant that night! He said they were late coming in because John had a nearly 200-pound halibut on the line. They rationalized the storm wouldn't be so bad so they stayed until they finally landed it. They were only a few hours from Salmon Beach. They heard about a man overboard in the area and were scanning the water for him on the way back, in spite of the storm. They were wearing their safety harnesses. The lanyards were clipped to the deck rings to minimize the possibility of being lost at sea. John even inflated their emergency life raft for the first time since owning the boat. They tied it aft but the way the wind and waves were behaving it was causing problems for the boat so they cut it loose. They figured they could find it the next day. Anyway, that is what Danny told Marlene."

Angela felt Sue was going into too much detail. "Sue, you said he saw Brant. What do you mean? Where? When? How?"

"I'm sorry. I just wanted to make sure I told you everything. Danny was on the boat's bow with a heavy-duty search light. He was scanning the ocean when he saw a man floating less than 100 feet away. It was right before the wave flipped their boat."

"Sue, do you have the number for the hospital? Can I call him? Now?"

"I knew you would want to talk to him. He is

receiving calls." Sue gave Angela the number and Danny answered the phone from his hospital room.

"Hello. Danny?"

"Yes." The voice sounded youthful but weak. Angela would have to be delicate.

"Danny, I am Angela Cormac, the wife of the man lost at sea the same night the Bella Bella went down. I'm so sorry about what happened to John and his brother-in-law but I'm so happy you are going to be OK."

"And I'm sorry for the loss of your husband," Danny replied. "That day will be a day of mourning for Salmon Beach for many years."

Angela related what Sue told her. Danny added that he managed to unsnap his harness but guessed the others had been knocked out and went down with the boat.

"Danny, is there anything else you can tell me? I heard you cut a life raft loose. Is it possible that Brant could have got to it?"

"I don't think so. We cut it loose at least 30 minutes before she sunk. I sure would have fared better if we had kept it with us though. I'm told I almost didn't make it."

"Were there supplies in the raft?" Angela felt she should find out all she could about this last hope that her husband was still alive.

"Yeah. John said it had candy bars, water, paddles, a radar gizmo for emergencies, even a sail."

"So if the wind and waves pushed Brant for a while it's possible he could have come upon it, right?"

Danny heard the desperation in Angela's voice.

"Sure, Mrs. Cormac. I think that's possible. But if he was out there longer than me…"

Angela interrupted. "He was wearing a dry suit so he could have lasted much longer. Anyway, thank you, Danny. I hope you are out of the hospital soon. Our place in Mexico is always available if you want some warmth."

"Thanks, Mrs. Cormac. Would you mind if I ask you a question?"

"Not at all. What is it?"

"Marlene and some of others told me about a rumor that your husband was taken out to sea by a humpback. Is what they are saying true? I mean, did you see a whale take him?"

"Yes, Danny. I did. I know it doesn't make sense but, well, I guess it doesn't matter since the whale spit him out."

"I didn't tell anyone this but…I can't be sure and I

don't know what good it does to even tell you what I thought. I…"

"Go ahead, Danny."

"I'm pretty sure I saw a whale that night in my light, just behind your husband, for a few seconds before I was slammed down."

Angela nearly fainted. She knew the whale was with Brant. Maybe it *still* was!

"Danny, I know this sounds crazy but I think that was the whale that took him. I think it still has him."

"Well, my nurse is here, Mrs. Cormac. I have to go. Please don't hesitate to call me for anything."

After Angela hung up she called the Ucluelet Coast Guard. The man who answered the phone recognized her voice immediately.

"Hello, Mrs. Cormac. How are you?"

"I just spoke with the man who survived the sinking of the Bella Bella. He's still in the hospital but is going to live. He said he saw Brant that night. He was alive. He also said he saw the whale. Most important, he said that nearly an hour to the south they cut a four-person life raft loose. There's a chance Brant might have found it. No one has searched that section of the ocean. Can you…"

The man interrupted. "Mrs. Cormac, even if he got to the raft, which is unlikely, how many days has it been now? Ten or 11? That close inland someone would have found him by now. He even could have sailed or paddled it to shore. I'm truly sorry. I can't send units out. I'll speak to the captain but I know what he'll say."

Angela told him she understood and hung up. She immediately called Dr. Stern. Akamu answered. Angela explained that she was coming to Maui in several days. She hoped that the tagged whale could be located by then.

Last Song of the Whales

16. The Decision

The next few days at sea allowed Brant to somewhat recover from his injuries and exhaustion. He had been thinking about the yellow antenna on Bluto's companion. He knew it must be a GPS device for tracking the whale. Brant tried to imagine the scientists who were following the whale knowing it was part of a group that included a man being pulled on a raft by a whale! He laughed to himself and realized it was the first time he had done so since being on the boat with his wife and friends. His laughter turned to tears as he realized they must believe him dead.

Brant was untying Boy each time they stopped. He trusted that Boy would not leave him and knew this allowed him the freedom to play during the group's rest times. Indeed, before and after each nap, Boy would roll, dive and breach. Today he jumped completely out of the water when Brant released the towline. He landed so close to the raft that the splash from his 40-foot long body almost filled it. Brant was exhausted trying to bail out the water. Then he noticed that five whales had joined in a circle less than 100 feet from him. They were making high-pitched noises and diving down. Brant saw a circle of bubbles coming straight up from where each whale dove. The bubbles apparently trapped hundreds of herring. Several seconds later the five whales surfaced with their giant mouths wide open and their flexible lower jaws puffed out. The precise moves of the whales amazed Brant. How such large creatures could do that without running into each other and with all getting a fair share of the food was remarkable. The whales repeated the maneuver. The first time they all ate fish. The second time all but the calf surfaced with closed mouths. Brant finally realized that they were not feeding but rather were teaching the calf this particular technique for catching fish.

The calf learned her lesson well, apparently. After the others bubble-netted the fish again, she took a mouthful and, expelling the sea water through her baleen filters, she slowly approached the raft. Reaching it, she opened her lower jaw under the raft and then flicked at least 100 herring into the boat. She nodded and rolled joyfully. Fish were jumping all over Brant as he tried to grab individual ones to eat. He thanked the calf and named her Charity. Brant felt he had captured enough rainwater in his jugs to digest the protein so he ate fish whole until his shrunken stomach was stuffed. He threw many overboard but kept enough for later.

The whales seemed pleased, waited for him to finish eating and then continued on their journey. Boy positioned himself alongside the raft so Brant could grab the line and retie it. After Brant secured the tow rope, his SART started beeping. Radar was nearby. Brant switched it to transponder mode. In a few minutes a ship came into view and was bearing down on his position fast. His heart soared with the prospect of being rescued. What a story he would have to tell his wife and the world. He got on his knees and began waving.

The ship was large, maybe 200-feet long, and steel gray above the copper-red hull. It had a huge foredeck, perhaps 20 feet above the main deck. It was connected to an access platform for the crew by a white metal bridge. In the center and at the bow sat what looked like a cannon. Three men stood beside it, one scouting and ready to operate the cannon. Below them, on both sides of the bow, the ship's name was painted in black letters, both in Japanese characters and in English. Brant soon could read the name "Yushin Maru." Brant realized it was a whaling ship. He could not imagine, however, that they would not be diverted by his plight. Maybe once aboard he could explain that the whales were, well, his friends. As soon as the thought came to him he understood how ridiculous it would sound even if there was someone who spoke English. Nonetheless, all he could think about was that he was going to be rescued!

He continued waving and yelling while Boy pulled him closer to the ship. Then he saw the men turn the cannon toward him. Brant realized he was putting Boy in harm's way. He released the line from the raft and shouted for Boy to dive. When the line was released, however, Boy simply stopped. First he looked at Brant then at the ship and then back at Brant. Brant screamed again for him to dive. To Brant's great relief Boy disappeared. Brant waved and yelled again at the ship. It could lower a line to him within minutes and he would be safe. Upon Boy's disappearance, however, the whaler turned sharply to the north. The captain apparently saw Bluto.

Brant could not believe the captain of a ship at sea would leave a man in a raft to chase a whale. Brant didn't know that just yesterday this ship had a run-in with the Sea Shepherd's 24-meter, high-tech, anti-whaling trimaran. The Sea Shepherd, an activist organization that had been committed to thwarting whaling operations on the open sea, had several ships and boats but the trimaran was its newest. Its new stealth boat was painted so it couldn't be recognized by radar and the previous day it had attempted to wrap a rope around the whaler's propeller. It almost succeeded but a second Japanese escort boat managed to fend off the trimaran. The Japanese must have thought Brant was one of the activist crew members who had remained to "guard" this group of whales.

The cannon exploded and Brant watched the harpoon launch into Bluto's side right in front of his dorsal fin. Brant set the oars and paddled with all of his might toward the ship. He was 100 feet from the bow when he heard Bluto's painful moan. He didn't see any blood in the water, so he assumed the harpoon didn't pierce any vital organs but Bluto wasn't moving. The crew quickly hauled him in with a powerful electric winch. By the time he reached the ship, Bluto came out of shock and attempted to dive but it was too late. The powerful crane lifted him up just enough to keep his head and blowholes under water. Bluto was struggling to get his head above water. Brant knew he was going to drown.

Brant screamed at the top of his lungs, cursing the ship and its crew. Amidships, two men were pulling a large hose off a reel. Brant figured they were going to spray him like he saw whalers do to Greenpeace protest boats. He quickly removed the flare gun and loaded one of the red cartridges from the strip of five. He fired it directly at the men with the hose. The flare hit the wall just above them and dropped on the deck, spinning and still on fire. The men dropped the hose and hid behind the hose reel. Brant loaded another shell and fired again. This one hit the cannon and bounced on the deck alongside one of the men, who immediately started slapping his pant leg to extinguish the smoldering material. All three ran back along the bridge and climbed down to the main deck. The ship turned suddenly, moved until it was half a mile from Brant and then stopped. Brant saw the crew return to the bow where they joined another group of men on the lower deck who were working to tether Bluto to the boat's side. Brant couldn't tell if Bluto was dead yet but he'd heard that many whales are butchered while still alive. Brant paddled toward them angrily but the ship sped away until it was but a dot on the horizon. He could not believe what had happened.

The captain had concluded that Brant was a member of the Sea Shepherd. Now that one of them had crossed the line, firing a weapon at the crew of an authorized ship, he would return to Japan to file legal complaints. He would put this activist group out of business permanently. Brant turned his SART off, removed the paddles and inserted them into the sail. He allowed the breeze to carry him away. He had made an important decision about his priorities that day.

Last Song of the Whales

17. The Clues

Angela arrived at Maui's Kahului Airport at 4:22
p.m., exactly two weeks and two days from when Brant
first disappeared into the jaws of a humpback whale. She
had left Zorro with a lady who lived near her casita. Julie
was an attractive trilingual lesbian who had lost her
longtime partner along with all the assets of the
unrecognized partnership. Living in the small Mexican
village with her parrot, she barely managed to support
herself. Brant and Angela had loaned her money and
encouraged her to continue her efforts to earn money as a
masseuse to Canadian tourists. She was an intelligent
woman with a great passion for animals and taking care
of Zorro was a win-win opportunity.

Akamu graciously met Angela at the airport with a
warm aloha and carried her bags to his old Toyota Celica.
He would drive her to her room at the Sun Seeker Hotel

in North Maui before taking her to Loni's office at the Pacific Whale Foundation. As they left the airport parking lot, Akamu warned Angela about the traffic delays they would encounter as a result of an environmental rally organized by students from the University of Hawaii's local community college and U.S. International University.

"A traffic jam in Maui is the last thing I would have expected," Angela said. She attempted to express a sense of humor, though her travel-weary energy made the comment sound more like a complaint.

"It is unusual but the students have managed to just about close down the town. They have been planning this for months and it really is important. In fact, Loni and I are involved. We are hoping to get some international media coverage."

"What's it about?" Angela asked politely although her mind obviously was on other things.

"It's about the plastic pollution surrounding the Hawaiian Islands. In 2006 the Hawaiian Islands National Wildlife Refuge was established inside the Papahānaumokuākea Marine National Monument. This is the largest Marine Protected Area in the world.

Unfortunately, it's becoming seriously polluted by the NPG. As a result many of our threatened species, like the green sea turtle, the Laysan albatross and the Hawaiian monk seal, are becoming endangered."

"What is the NPG?" Angela asked.

"I'm sorry. That stands for the North Pacific Gyre. It's a slowly moving spiral of currents created by a high pressure system of air currents. There are four other gyres worldwide that are major dumps. The two in the NPG are the Eastern and Western Garbage Patches. The plastic polymers act like sponges and soak up pesticides and other poisons, like PCBs, a million times the level in the water. Jellyfish and other creatures eat it and the poison makes its way up the food chain. We also have beaches that were pristine several years ago. Now they are full of plastic trash fragments, sometimes a foot deep."

Angela shook her head. "I heard about an island of plastic between the U.S. and Hawaii. My husband taught environmental science at the University of Arizona. We would see plastic on the ocean all the time in Mexico and Canada. Brant said there are 50,000 pieces of plastic for every square mile of ocean. I think that statistic came from the United Nations."

Akamu did not want to talk about Angela's husband. He believed he was dead. Besides, his people had a saying, "To the living we owe respect, to the dead we owe the truth." So he continued with the story about the demonstration.

"You know the plastic isn't good for the whales either and the people here hold the whales dear to their hearts. In the past few months there have been scattered reports about several mysterious species of whales beaching themselves in different places around the world. An autopsy was performed on a 24-foot whale that beached itself near Greenland. The researchers found six square meters of plastic debris in its stomach. The U.S. is doing nothing about the plastic problem but a few cities and even China just banned free plastic bags."

It took them about an hour to get past the marchers with all of their signs. Students had created art work from the colorful plastic. There also were posters with horrible images of mammal and bird skeletons with their bellies full of plastic. When they arrived at the hotel, Akamu waited while Angela checked in, dropped off her luggage and freshened up. Then they went to see Loni. Akamu introduced them and went home. After a cordial greeting and some small talk about the flight and the student march, Angela launched into her overly rehearsed speech. It was an effort to solicit help from Loni and to somehow organize a new search party for Brant.

"Dr. Stern, please just listen to my logic for starting a new search. A humpback whale takes Brant into its mouth and carries him out to sea. This alone is so strange it should make any whale researcher want to learn more about this whale and its motivation. Then the whale spits him out but a witness sees the whale with him hours later. So we can presume the whale has some reason to be with my husband and that they may still be together. We know a life raft with food, water, a sail and oars was let loose in the same vicinity where Brant had been. It is possible he found it. The raft had a sailing rig and he knows how to sail. He might be heading downwind to Hawaii on the same route as the migrating whale that has the tracking device pinned to it.

"So if we go to where the GPS shows your whale is we MIGHT find my whale and my husband, no?

Angela waited for Loni's response. Unfortunately it confirmed her fears. These pieces of logic were far stretches of the imagination with low scientific probabilities. Even if she wanted, Loni said she couldn't use this line of reasoning to convince the university, the foundation or anyone else to finance a search. She would be happy to show Angela around the research facility and photos of whales and look at the tracking chart for the tagged whale. In the morning, however, she had to fly to Honolulu to teach a class. She was sorry Angela had traveled so far to hear her disappointing news.

Angela politely refused Loni's offer for the tour. She had expected this reaction in her head but in her heart she felt it would turn out differently. She would try to find someone with a private boat or airplane in the morning.

Around 9:30 p.m. Akamu received a telephone call from a friend, a Japanese student named Baku, who was working toward his doctorate in marine biology at the University of British Columbia. His interest in whales often brought him into contact with Akamu. They were interns together under Loni's mentorship. Baku was serving as a volunteer researcher on the whaling ship that had been fired upon by a guy in a life raft. He recalled the entire story of what happened and how terrible it was for him to witness the killing of a beautiful humpback whale. It was the first one he ever saw killed by a whaler.

It was not unusual for Japanese whaling ships to bring researchers on board even if one of the team happened to be aligned with the anti-whaling movement. They wanted scientists aboard to support their claims that they were hunting whales solely for research. A report from a whale activist confirming this would be helpful. Of course, the crew had orders to put on a show when observers were aboard. Although Article VIII of the International Convention for the Regulation of Whaling (ICRW) specifically provided for its members to kill whales for research and to process and sell the by-products, authentic research was rare.

Baku told Akamu that at first they thought the man was with the Sea Shepherd's crew. He said they had a run-in with them the previous day. Baku said that secretly he had been rooting for them to disable the whaling ship and it seemed likely until another Japanese boat came to the rescue and chased the trimaran away. He told Akamu that he recently learned the man was not with the Sea Shepherd and wondered who it could have been. He confessed to feeling badly about leaving an innocent man at sea in a lifeboat but was himself confused about why the man shot at the whaler if he wasn't with the whales.

Akamu could not believe what he was hearing.

"Baku, what you have told me is very important. I think this is the man we're looking for. His wife is here. It is an unbelievable story. I will tell you about it later. First I must call Loni. It is amazing you saw this. Thank you for telling me. I'll call you back."

Akamu hung up the phone and called Loni at her office and home but she wasn't at either place. Then he called the hotel and asked for Angela. When she answered, he told her what he knew. Angela insisted he call his friend back to ask what the man was wearing. Akamu called her back 20 minutes later and said the man was in a small orange raft, unusual for the Sea Shepherd team. He was wearing a black wet or dry suit and a yellow life vest.

18. The Plan

Early the next morning, Akamu picked up Angela and headed for an emergency meeting that Loni arranged after she confirmed the story about the sighting of the man by the Japanese student. The trio walked into the office of the Pacific Whale Foundation's director, Dr. Jeff Morrow, at 9 a.m. A member of the U.S. Coast Guard's Maui station and a representative from Maui Marine Services (MMS) also were in the room. MMS was a private company that did marine salvage and search and rescue. Everyone greeted her with the traditional "aloha nui loa." Loni, introduced by Dr. Morrow as "Dr. Loni Stern," began the discussion.

"Thank you very much for coming to this meeting on such short notice. As I told some of you on the telephone, I just learned about a man on a life raft who shot flares at the Yushin Maru two days ago. I feel that, in light of the extraordinary factors in this case, the possibility that Professor Cormac might be the man involved cannot be ignored. We have the coordinates from the captain of the whaler as to where the incident occurred. He kept them for a lawsuit against the Sea Shepherd group. He since has been informed that the man was not affiliated with that organization. I already spoke with Captain Paul Watson, who was on the Sea Shepherd's new trimaran. He confirmed that the first he knew of the man was yesterday morning. He said he'd be willing to help find him. He might be able to go back to the area in a few days after some necessary repairs are made to the trimaran's electronic equipment.

"I also learned something else. The coordinates I received from the Japanese whaler captain and the trimaran match a signal location within 20 miles of one of our tagged whales. It's a whale we suspect this man might have been following."

"Why do you think the man was following your whale?" Jeff asked. He was a busy man and didn't want to waste time.

"I'm sorry. I should have explained." Loni knew this was a weak link in her argument. "The whale that took

Mr., I mean Dr. Cormac, apparently was enroute to our islands. As you know, over 10,000 whales migrate here annually. Most of the others probably left at least two weeks before, except for one of our tracked whales, which left around the same time as the one in question. The whales often gather in small groups for the voyage. If we find our tagged whale there is a good chance we also will find Dr. Cormac, if indeed he is alive and miraculously being somehow tended to by a whale pod."

The Coast Guard captain sighed. He was in charge of Station Maui. Its operation was under the control of Coast Guard Sector Honolulu. It had 24 crew members with one 47-foot life boat and a 25-foot response boat. The station stayed busy year-round performing search and rescue, pollution response and marine mammal enforcement, especially within the Hawaiian Humpback Whale Sanctuary. He sighed because he simply did not believe the man was alive or with whales.

"Even if he was in the raft, I don't see, and excuse me, ma'am, for being so blunt," the captain looked at Angela, "how it is possible for your husband to be alive even if he had managed to acquire the small life raft with the sail. Hell, sailing across the Pacific with such an emergency rig would be something for the record books. If miraculously he was able to keep up with the whales and use their navigation skills—also highly unlikely on many counts—he could not live for three weeks on what was in it. As for that fellow shooting at the whaling ship, he was surely one of those anti-whaling activists. They are denying it for obvious reasons. What he did was illegal, maybe even attempted murder on the high seas."

He continued, "Also our jurisdiction is 500 square miles around the islands. Going offshore 700 miles, where the coordinates showed the man and the whale to be, is out of our range. Even if I felt the search was warranted I'd have to get permission from D.C."

Loni responded, "If the man has survived this long, I mean it's been over two weeks, he already has been resourceful enough to figure out how to live off the sea. We are willing to wait four more days, which would allow us to better track his location and put him closer to us. At the rate the whales usually travel, this would put him within about 400 miles of here."

Angela was shocked to hear that Loni was suggesting waiting.

"We can't wait," she said. "Each day that passes

decreases his chances for survival. We need to go first thing in the morning or today."

The man from the private company spoke next.

"Four hundred miles is a lot of ocean, you know. Your whale has a tag but a GPS doesn't work on whales the way it does on land. The unit is never dry enough for a satellite to triangulate a signal. So your tag, even if it is state-of-the-art, transmits to the satellite but the satellite has to analyze positions using a Doppler shift. It is not very accurate. It is going to take some serious calculating to come close to where he might be now."

The director interjected, as if defending his tag devices. "You are right to a point. These whale tags are not as accurate as we would like but should easily get us within airplane viewing range. That's why I don't think this is a boat search and rescue. It will require an airplane."

Angela, excited things were moving in a positive direction, jumped in. "Don't forget there is supposed to be a radar device on the raft. That also will help locate him."

"Yes," Loni spoke. "The Japanese captain mentioned they saw the signal from a responder. Thinking it was a boat from the Sea Shepherd they paid it no mind."

"This is what I suggest. Mrs. Cormac has indicated a willingness to pay for private services so I'll leave that to her and MMS to negotiate. Meanwhile I'll speak with my board of directors to see if the Foundation can contribute in a way that relates to our research. And captain, if you would check with D.C. to see what you can do, that would be great. Dr. Stern, if you and Mrs. Cormac would check back tomorrow around this time I'll have my secretary field you all the information we have."

The meeting ended and Loni, Akamu and Angela drove to a local restaurant for lunch. Akamu ordered a plate of fried shrimp. Angela could not help but comment in spite of always chastising Brant when he did so.

"Akamu, have you read my husband's book about shrimp farms and trawling? The only way we can stop the terrible pollution and by-catch is to boycott shrimp. If everyone stopped eating shrimp our oceans, fisheries, groundwater and mangrove swamps no longer would be polluted by the antibiotics and pesticides used in shrimp farming. Our ocean bottom habitats and other fisheries would not be being destroyed by trawlers."

Akamu knew what she was talking about but he was

conscious of how difficult it would be to change the public's eating habits.

Angela felt bad and offered an apology. "I'm sorry, Akamu. I always hated it when Brant would do what I just did to friends. I had no right."

"No. You had every right. I have learned my lesson."

He called the waitress back and changed his order to a red snapper sandwich. He knew everything had a price and probably nothing was really completely safe to eat anymore but the shrimp problem was hurting the oceans and its creatures in a very significant way.

After lunch they went to the tracking station to see the course plotting for the tagged whale. Curiously, the whale had turned away from its most direct route to the islands. It appeared to be heading northwest. Loni knew this could throw off the search's timing and accuracy if they were lucky enough to get the go ahead.

19. The Gyre

Several days passed since the whaling incident. Brant felt as if a physical, mental and spiritual metamorphosis had transformed him into a different being. He chanted a song which he learned from the Oglala when he had visited the Pine Ridge Indian Reservation. It was one he sang in his Mexican temescal. As he sang, he felt the power of the untranslatable sounds in a way that made him feel truly alive and connected to the great mysterious world he was in. His body's molecules blended with the sea and sky and everything they encompassed. He had no regrets about his decision to follow the whales.

Brant's ability to navigate was growing and he realized that he and the whales had been traveling northwest for some time. He wondered if the whales had gone off course to avoid something. Of course Brant knew questioning a whale's ability to navigate was like questioning a fire's ability to burn.

Brant had read extensively about the humpback's navigation skills. Although whale researchers knew very little about how the humpbacks found their way from Canada to the small chain of islands more than 3,000 miles away, there was no doubt about their ability to do so. Some humpbacks migrated more than 5,000 miles from Central America to feeding grounds near Antarctica. It is the longest migration of any mammal.

Of course the scientists had their hypotheses. One likely possibility was that the whales might use biomagnetic navigation. They used the earth's magnetic field to cross oceans similar to how many birds find their way across the skies. The strength of the field varies with lower and higher ranges, much like the landscape's hills and valleys. A substance called biomagnetite that researchers found in humpback brains seemed to play a role in this ability to discern magnetic fields. Others believe that the whales—humpbacks and other species— use multiple ways to navigate, such as echolocation. Emitting loud sounds at low frequencies allows them to locate islands or other prominent underwater features by bouncing the sound off it and waiting for the rebounding echo.

Some scientists believe humpback calves simply remember their first voyage with their mother. It is unusual for them to deviate from the course taken the previous year. The close relationship between mothers and calves offered more evidence that considerable knowledge is transferred from mother to baby. In fact, a few scholars believed that this learning included celestial and astrological navigation, using the sun, moon and stars with a type of internal sextant.

The songs themselves also may be a way humpbacks navigate. Brant knew that Boy and the others' constant singing had many purposes, one of them being navigation. Now, more than ever, he felt those who believed only male humpbacks sang when breeding were wrong. Certainly Bluto's singing did not elicit a romantic response from Charity's mother.

Brant wondered if Indigenous tribes might have used songs to navigate away from the whales. His interest in Indigenous ways of knowing had brought him to study the Lakota and the Seri Indians. Along with Dr. Lorri Monti of Northern Arizona University's Center for Sustainable Environments, Brant spent several weeks recording Seri Indian navigation songs in their village near Bahia de Kino in Sonora near Tiburon Island. They were no longer being used and were at risk of being lost forever when the last of the elders who remembered them died.

The songs were similar to Aboriginal song lines. They offered complex ways to identify landmarks. Sometimes they told stories about a specific area that related to a landmark. Other times, the song's tone or rhythm gave clues as to time and distance. For the Aboriginals, who used the songs for land navigation, walking the wrong way along a song line would be considered a serious and disrespectful mistake. Geographic features on earth were alive and sacred. Brant now believed the whales felt the same way about the oceanscape. In the Seri songs, interpreters explained how many features of the coast and the islands were described in the lyrics. By singing the songs in the right order, they could navigate long distances in their ocean canoes. Brant was convinced that many of the songs the whales had been singing were used the same way.

Brant's thoughts on navigation were inspired by the beauty and serenity of the morning, which, like the previous two days, offered calm seas and sunny skies. He looked around, squinting in the sunlight, and noticed that more whales were everywhere in the distance. They were coming from every direction. By late afternoon he estimated he saw over 500 whales of different species. They all were heading in the same direction he was traveling.

Just before dusk Brant noticed the water was turning from blue and green to a brownish red. This was the "red tide" about which he had learned more than he wanted to know while living at his coastal residences. Brant looked into the water. Something was different about this algae bloom. It looked like vegetable soup except instead of vegetables it was full of colorful particles of plastic, plastic bags and various other plastic objects. The plastic debris continued as far down as he could see.

Seeing plastic in the ocean was nothing new for Brant. After all, he lived on two coasts. Several days north of his Mexico home, the Seri Indian village was full of plastic that often blew into the ocean. At first, he was horrified by the site of hundreds of bags of plastic strewn through the Seri village on the coast just across from Tiburon, the sacred and largest island in the Sea of

Cortez.

There only were about 900 Seri left. They referred to themselves as "Kun-kaak." Brant once thought their knowledge and respect for the sea made their apparent disregard for the plastic a terrible contradiction. Maybe he still did but he understood the situation better after living with them for awhile. There was no money for garbage collection. They barely managed to have water to drink. Most lived in open shanties made of discarded sheets of wood or siding. The food they managed to get from the nearest town, two rough hours away on an often washed out sandy road, came in plastic bags. Over the years, with no place to put it and no way to bury it, they let it accumulate. After all, for thousands of years they only used natural, biodegradable products. As long as the plastic did not get into the ocean where was the harm? They were more concerned with plants and animals brought into the region that were not indigenous to it.

Of course, the Seri were wrong. The plastic bags eventually did make their way into the ocean. They and most everyone else had become used to seeing plastic bags floating in the sea but no one could have imagined something like the vast accumulation Brant had come upon. He knew he must be in the infamous "plastic garbage patch." The flat water and absence of a breeze was further evidence. He was in a vortex where four prevailing ocean currents met in a rotational pattern that drew in waste from the coastal waters of North America and Asia and trapped the floating debris. He heard estimates of its size ranging from twice the area of Texas to the size of the entire continental United States. But why had the whales taken him here? For that matter why were so many whales coming here?

Night came quickly. Brant untied Boy and listened to the silence of the doldrums. It was quiet except for a growing wailing that did not allow Brant to sleep. It was an eerie, melancholy sound that began with a few whales but by midnight had turned into a chorus of many. It was a tragic repetition of moans.

Last Song of the Whales

20. The Mystery

Throughout the night Brant listened to the whales' breathing and mournful singing, unable to sleep. In the light of dawn he saw that more whales had arrived. They seemed to be feeding but not in any way he'd ever observed. They were skimming the top 6 to 10 feet of the ocean with their mouths wide open, never diving. Some groups formed military-like rows, side to side and touching one another. Perfectly synchronized, they vacuumed the debris for a mile before changing direction. Brant was shocked and baffled by their intentions and the methodical process they used.

Brant had been paddling around, looking at the larger items in the garbage. He thought there might be something he could use. When he saw a six pack of plastic apple juice containers he felt like a child who found an Easter egg. He removed the plastic wrapping and stuffed it in his dry suit, as if it would make a difference. Small straws were attached to each package. There were pointed ends for sticking into an aluminum covered hole at the top of the four-ounce package. Anxious for a taste of the sweet fluid, he carefully sipped but found the juice had turned to vinegar. It still quenched his thirst however. Brant slowly drank the rest, chasing it with a little water.

He located a 6-foot wooden pole, still in good shape. If he could find some fishing line, maybe even a hook, he could make a lure to catch some fish. He would need food. He was almost out of nutrition bars and whatever sardines remained in the puddles of ocean water at the bottom of his raft were no longer edible. The small amount of nylon line on the raft was not long enough. While he was looking for something suitable he passed a gill net and cursed at it. Then he paddled to a large box with Chinese characters on it. He used the pole to smash open the sealed lid. Inside were brand new military style bayonets. Brant took one and threw it into the raft. He made sure his pod was still nearby. He thought it was interesting that he used the word "pod." Yes, he was part of a whale pod, he thought. On the way back he encountered a snarled longline with large hooks. He cut off about 30 feet that seemed usable and one of the hooks that was within his reach.

In the calm water, the plastic debris reflected the sunlight in many directions with rainbow-like colors streaming out just under the surface. Boy, Charity, Charity's mother and the adult male were not participating in the insane feeding. They still were floating next to one another near the raft. Brant could see the yellow plastic signaling device clearly on the older male's back and paddled over for a closer look. He thought it would be best if the device was on his raft if it was to aid in his rescue. It also would work better out of the water. He knew it only could transmit signals when the whale was on the surface. The whale remained remarkably still as Brant maneuvered himself and the raft into position. Using all his strength he managed to remove the unit from the whale's blubber. Then he tied it to the flare box in his raft so the antenna was pointing up.

Several minutes later the whale, relieved to no longer have the transmitter in him, slowly swam away. It uttered a series of wide-ranging pitches that the others repeated as if sharing a farewell message. Twenty yards away he opened his mouth, scooped up tons of water and garbage, squeezed the water out through his baleen and swallowed the contents. He continued swimming with the vacuuming motion. The calf's mother bid her farewell and dove out of sight. Brant watched for several minutes. She blew 100 yards to the north and began the same eating ritual.

Brant looked at Boy.

"Oh no you don't! Don't even think about it!" Brant paddled alongside Boy. He picked up the towline and tied it to the raft. "Come on. Let's get out of here!"

To his relief, Boy and Charity headed back on course. After nearly an hour of passing hundreds, maybe thousands, of whales of numerous species, all engaged in eating the plastic garbage, Boy began eating, too.

"Stop it!" Brant yanked the line tied to his fin and shouted repeatedly but Boy continued swimming forward, constantly swallowing the debris after straining out the seawater. Brant couldn't stop him. He splashed water and screamed at the whale but Boy ignored his pleas.

Brant studied the smooth ocean that surrounded him. Floating on the surface and just below it was every plastic product imaginable. There were all sorts of plastic bags. He could still read many of the store names, such as Sears, Bristol Farms, El Pollo Loco, Fred Meyer and Taco Bell. He saw toys, medical waste products, packing straps, deodorant bottles, Ziploc bags and millions of small plastic pellets. The list was endless. He even saw a nutrition bar wrapper and remembered with extreme guilt that the wind had blown one of his out of the raft the previous week.

Boy's cruising speed was a steady three or four knots, even while sucking in water and plastic. The pace, however, must have been too slow for Charity. Now, independent of her mother, she decided to go it alone. She increased her speed, cavorted in circles for awhile and then disappeared. Brant noticed she never ate the plastic. He thought this was strange since she usually copied the adults' behavior. Could it be this horrible gathering was meant to save the younger generation from death by plastic and the young had been told not to eat it? He had heard that many fish, birds, dolphins and whales were dying from the high amounts of plastic they were ingesting by accident or because plastic particles appeared as plankton. Maybe the whales were sacrificing themselves and trying to vacuum up the plastic from what seemed to be the source here in this vortex.

Boy and Brant continued traveling through the plastic and whales for the rest of the day. Not all the whales were eating. Many were dead and floating in various positions. The sun was hot and Brant used the sail for shade while he tried to make sense of what he saw. Boy rested only twice all day and into the night but Brant fell asleep under a vast array of bright stars and planets pinned to the dark, bluish-black sky. Somewhere around three or four a.m. Brant bolted upright, unable to breathe. He gasped for air and looked around before realizing he had been dreaming. He didn't usually remember his dreams. During the past several days, however, they came to him each morning with great clarity. This was not his first nightmare. It was the first one to wake him.

In his dream he saw a whale breach straight out of the water. Instead of turning to splash back down, it continued straight up into the starry night. Its flukes propelled it through the air like it was swimming. Brant was magically riding the whale but struggling to hold on. His grip was loosening and he fell back toward earth and the sea. The whale continued upward. Just before crashing into the ocean, the sun came out and revealed a thick, red-brown liquid where the blue ocean had been. As the whale continued going up, Brant saw himself running in the air like a cartoon character, trying to avoid landing in the mucky water. Then he fell downward and splashed through the surface. He was covered in the reddish mixture of plants and plastic that was too thick for him to penetrate and it held him under. He kept trying to break through and was about to run out of air. Strangely, there was a large piece of plastic, perhaps some type of bottle, he could see through. He looked up and saw the whale surrounded by stars, except now it had become half-man—a whale-man.

Brant was amazed by the detail of his dream and his ability to remember it so clearly. He looked at the stars, half expecting to see the whale-man there. He noticed the constellations had moved to the opposite side of the sky. To the east the sun's first rays had erased the stars, pushing a light breeze toward the west. Brant was hungry and thirsty. He ate a nutrition bar, making sure he placed the wrapper safely inside the box. His water supply had dwindled down to a quart. Eating the fish Charity gave him helped to somewhat quench his thirst but with six or seven more days ahead of him, Brant wouldn't survive without more water. Without rain he would die.

In spite of his poor prospects, Brant couldn't stop thinking about his dream about the whale-man and how it might relate to the tragedy he witnessed while in the vortex. What were the whales doing? Brant went through all the possibilities he could imagine. He knew the whales weren't hungry. They just left their feeding grounds and were on their way to the breeding grounds. Food in the gyre is minimal anyway and they certainly would know that. Regardless, the manner in which they were eating was abnormal. Brant had no doubt they were intentionally trying to eat or "kill" the plastic. It also was rare to see different species of whales together. Perhaps these whales knew better than the world's scientists exactly what the plastic pollution with all its chemicals was doing to the oceans and future generations of whales and other creatures. If 100,000 or more whales consumed a ton of plastic every day for several weeks it surely would have an effect on the situation. They might have even thought such a suicidal effort would motivate humans to use their powers to finish the job if they knew what the whales were doing.

There was a problem, however. The whales were wrong about the gyre. There were not enough whales to destroy all the plastic. Nor was the gyre the source of it. They also were wrong about thinking that consuming it would eliminate it from the ocean. It all would return when their bodies decomposed. They didn't seem to know what Brant understood about the result of so many large bodies decomposing around the same time. The large number of shark carcasses from the longline fishing was already creating decreased amounts of oxygen in the waters along the longline path. Brant thought the death of so many whales might create a condition so serious that earth's atmospheric oxygen would diminish dangerously.

Brant was playing with all the puzzle pieces. Most people did not believe whales could be this premeditating or calculating. He would have a difficult time convincing people of what he thought the whales were trying to accomplish. Before being taken to sea by the whale, Brant might also have said such cognitive abilities were not possible. After being with them for these weeks, however, he no longer doubted that their intelligence was sufficient to attempt such a solution. He was even beginning to wonder if he had been taken to witness their plan.

Brant argued against his own hypothesis, playing the devil's advocate. If the whales were smart enough to try and destroy the plastic, why weren't they smart enough to know the plastic would return when their bodies decayed? Surely they had seen birds and mammals' skeletons filled with plastic on beaches, floating on the water or at the bottom of the sea. Maybe they also knew that humans were the source of the plastic and not the gyre itself! They might even know that there was far too much plastic to be able to clean it up, no matter how many whales were involved. If the whales somehow knew this, then how could thousands of dying whales out of sight of humans possibly stop the production of plastic that was poisoning the oceans? Could the whales—with their intelligence and introspective abilities—believe that their actions would prompt appropriate human intervention? But how would people know? Could his being on the scene also be part of some plan?

Brant's contemplations ended abruptly when 200 feet away a large sailfish soared from the water. Brant forced himself to stop thinking and merely breathe the clean ocean air deep into his lungs. Life was amazing, he thought. In spite of his predicament and the mystery at hand, he must not lose sight of the beauty that surrounded him. He remembered his fishing gear and began rigging it up. He didn't want to catch anything as big as a sailfish but maybe he could snag a small fish with a piece of herring or using one of the plastic lures he picked up at the gyre.

Brant shook his head in disbelief about all that was happening to him and smiled. Here he was, fishing in the middle of the Pacific Ocean, being transported by whale power. No one would believe it.

Brant was not getting any bites and his mind quickly returned to the problems he had been considering. He had been a professional researcher in the university system for 20 years. He specialized in environmental science and Indigenous wisdom. He just wrote a book about shrimp farms and how the pesticides and antibiotics used to kill a virus in the shrimp crop were causing eutrophication of the oceans and decreasing its oxygen. He wondered if he could create a theory explaining the whales' actions that he could offer to the authorities that would not make them think he was insane.

Brant began his hypothesis with the plankton cycle.

He wondered about the relationship between whales and the harmful algal blooms. For starters whale dung is a source of nutrition for phytoplankton. Whales eat zooplankton that feeds on phytoplankton. So what? If fish die and are not recycled in the food chain they decay at the ocean's bottom. Bacterial decomposition removes valuable oxygen from the water, causing hypoxia or dead zones. No life. No plankton. No oxygen. One way the whales participate in the symbiotic system of nature is eating the fish before they go to the bottom, resulting in no bacterial decomposition. The more living creatures in the oceans the more balanced the exchange between oxygen and carbon. Without the whales that balance would be upset. This imbalance would be far more obvious than that being caused by the plastic at this time.

From this line of reasoning, Brant concluded that the whales were indeed committing suicide to force an imbalance that somehow would compel humans to start paying attention to their destruction of the ocean. Maybe they weren't trying to destroy the plastic at all. Perhaps they only wanted to kill themselves. Brant knew other creatures, like certain moths, committed suicide or prevented reproduction when their instincts predicted insufficient food or other dangers for future generations. Maybe this was an advanced intelligence doing the same thing.

Brant thought he had a nibble on the line but it did not take the plastic bait in its mouth. But he was definitely getting bites.

Brant started over with his hypothesis. If the whales were attempting to stop humans from destroying the world—whether or not that involved plastic—what could come of their deaths other than getting bleeding heart activists to complain? What would be big enough to match the importance of their actions? How would people know if most of the whales died at sea? There already were numerous mysterious beachings and it seemed no one was doing much to learn why.

Brant thought about a phrase that a scientist named Hsu used to describe the ocean during the mass extinction of the dinosaurs. He called it a "Strangelove ocean," referring to the doomsday machine used in the movie *Dr. Strangelove.* Hsu wrote that something, maybe an asteroid, had caused the sudden death of many of the sea-living animals. Removing a large percentage of marine life released a high amount of carbon dioxide into the atmosphere. Brant remembered that research showed that following the dinosaur extinction, the atmosphere's CO_2 levels were so high it took millions of years until enough sea creatures returned to draw the CO_2 back to a life-sustaining level. So…

Fish were no longer hitting at the plastic lure but it was still on the line as it bounced along the surface 30 feet or so behind the raft.

Brant continued with his idea that if enough whales died they would represent a large segment of sea life's oxygen absorbing ability. If their bodies decomposed, they also would play a large role in sending off CO_2 gases. My God, Brant thought, the whales were around before, during and after the extinction. If they did possess great intelligence, knowledge and wisdom, they might know more about this history and understand all this far better than he or any scientists!

If his scenario had any validity—especially if the whales were doing the same thing at plastic garbage heaps worldwide—their effort could be the last straw. It could cause the kind of catastrophic event needed to create another Strangelove ocean. After all, for over 500 years, humans have been setting the stage. Global warming was one indication of rising CO_2 rates in the atmosphere the same way HABs revealed lower oxygen rates in the ocean. The plastic itself, with its ability to absorb poisonous gases and return them to the air, also might be a contributing factor.

Brant felt another tug on his line, then a hit and then nothing. He returned to his thoughts. He was thinking about several articles written by one of his favorite marine researchers, Debbie MacKenzie. She was the director of the Gray Seal Conservation Society and a prolific author of scientific articles about the Strangelove ocean. She had written that fossil records in ocean sediment revealed that unusual plankton blooms were prominently featured. They were quite similar to those that were proliferating globally in recent years. She argued that extracting life from the sea in bulk had induced rising atmospheric CO_2 and declining oxygen. Brant would love to ask her what she thought would happen if thousands of whales all died within or under one year.

She talked about a subtle "biological forcing" or active control of plankton growth by larger animals. The effects of this erosion weren't being considered by those who believed the oceans were limitless resources. In one of her lectures that Brant attended she said, "We think we can have our fish and eat it too."

Brant knew that anyone who spent time on the sea would agree that there were far fewer fish than a mere decade ago. Dr. MacKenzie also had interesting evidence to support her argument. Records indicated a time when the atmosphere's rising CO_2 levels stopped rising abruptly. Ironically, it happened during World War II when CO_2 emissions should have been at their highest. Brant remembered her answer well. She said that fishing, sealing and whaling almost stopped completely! As she put it, a "biological carbon pump" in the sea recouped some of its former strength and momentum while the fishermen were fighting in the war.

Brant felt another hit on the line and then a pull. A small dorado, maybe three feet long, had taken the bait. It danced magically on the surface as Brant started rolling the line up the pole by turning it on the pole. He knew he had to keep the hook from pulling out of the fish's mouth. He set the pole down and began pulling the line in with his bare hands. The line cut into his palms but he kept the tension. The fish was on tight. Brant's best bet was to haul it in by hand as fast as he could. He pulled the line hand over hand with all his strength until the blue and green fish was in the raft. He immediately held him up by the tail and then plunged his knife into the back of its head. The fish fluttered and died. Brant offered a thank you blessing and began drinking the blood straight from the dorado's wounds. He was about to have a sashimi dinner.

Catching the fish was no small feat. Brant knew it may have been a temporary reprieve from certain death. The fish blood had only one-third of the salt contained in sea water and would sustain Brant for another few days. He savored every bite, settled back, and reflected again on Dr. MacKenzie's research and his own.

Brant knew whales held a special position in the plankton cycle because of the vast amounts of zooplankton they consumed. Dr. MacKenzie had measured the amount of carbon in baleen whales, using isotope ratios, something that was way beyond Brant's expertise. She used that to create a history of how well the plankton was doing in terms of oxygen/carbon exchanges. All Brant understood was that she believed this process could predict a second Strangelove ocean.

Returning to his own observations that there was a relationship between the HABs, abnormally high atmospheric CO_2 and hypoxic oceans, Brant started to believe the whales might intentionally be creating the conditions for another mass extinction.

Brant couldn't help but think of all the talk about the end of the Mayan calendar on December 21, 2012. That day was supposed to mark either the beginning of a new age of harmony or the end of human life. Was it possible such an event would occur in another two years? He doubted it. If there was any truth to the 2012 prophesies, it marked a cycle of evolution rather than a single point in time. One could not discount the fact, however, that humans were rapidly destroying life systems on earth. Something radical must happen to wake people up. What if what the whales were doing with the plastic was that something? Regardless, if another mass extinction was close at hand humans had to know about its possibility and immediately take action.

The whales, sharks, fish and other ocean creatures were engaged in a complex interaction with the photosynthesis of phytoplankton. System balance required diversity and significant biomass. The absence of a large number of whales alone could tip the scales but combined with the bacterial decomposition of their immense bodies, the process would be exponentially worse. Brant knew that humans could suffocate when the atmosphere's oxygen levels reached 19.5 percent. Sure, elite mountain climbers and people living at high altitudes might survive. Most of us would not. Currently the planet was at 20.9 percent. This was an all time low if the atmosphere for the millions of years preceding and following the mass extinctions of 60 million years ago wasn't included. There was no question that the oceans were suffering from anoxia with increasing numbers of dead zones and individuals with respiratory disorders, like asthma. Just before going out on the boat with Angela, Sue and Gilles, Brant had read where Japan had recently been invaded by giant jellyfish all along its coast. Fishermen there claimed they had never seen so many. Similar reportings were happening around the world. Brant knew jellyfish did well in warmer, polluted, deoxygenated waters, like those being created by the climate change phenomenon. Even if people did not die from an inability to breathe, they could not function properly. The result would be an inability to maintain normal life.

Brant broke the dorado's spine and was sucking out the bone's contents. The liquid inside was minimal but he needed every little bit possible to survive. He ate as much as he could, then put the remainder of the fish in the shadiest portion of the raft.

21. The Signal

The morning after Angela's meeting with the Coast Guard, the Whale Foundation and the private company, she called Loni to see what decisions, if any, had been made. Loni was not around so she left a message on her machine and called Akamu. He didn't answer either. She waited in her room for several hours, mindlessly flicking through equally mindless television programs. By 11 a.m. Loni called Angela back. She said the Whale Foundation's board members did not feel they could adequately rationalize the cost of a search venture. They apologized. The Coast Guard, however, was more hopeful. Honolulu had the only suitable airplane and the headquarters there needed permission from Washington, D.C. The chain of command in Washington probably would require at least another day before making a decision. Apparently an admiral was involved and he was checking with the Japanese government on the details surrounding the whaler.

"Don't they know this is an emergency? Would they have to go through all of this if someone called to say a boat went down and there was one survivor at sea? Come on. We have witnesses. It must have been Brant the whalers saw. We should have been out there yesterday! Damn it. I'll find someone to fly me and the hell with all of you."

As soon as Angela hung up the phone she was sorry. Loni, however, immediately called back.

"Look, Mrs. Stern, I understand. I even agree with you. I started to tell you that for $3,000 MMS will leave early the next morning if you want, weather permitting."

"Yes, yes. I want to go. How will they have access to the tagged whale's route?"

Loni didn't tell Angela that the tagged whale previously went off course. Now she explained that she was late in calling because she was checking the tracking for the whale. For some reason the whale went off course but now was heading in the right direction. This could have presented problems. Humpbacks usually don't go so far off their normal routes. Sure, they make smaller detours for various reasons but not a full day in a different direction.

Loni continued, "The signals, however, are unusual."

"What do you mean?" Angela interrupted, expecting bad news.

"The transmitter only sends a signal to the ARGOS satellite when the whale surfaces. The signal can't go through the water. The satellite circles the earth every 100 minutes so it is only over one place roughly 10 minutes during each rotation. There often are days when we don't receive any signal. Actually getting a daily reading is rare. This is one reason our foundation was reluctant to search for the man in the raft, even though the Coast Guard's resources would cover a larger area. By the way, I think they are going to say yes. I also heard that whoever shot the flares might be charged with some sort of felony at sea.

Loni chose her words carefully. Angela did not need more stress.

"I believe they consider this to be a legitimate search and rescue mission. Using the Japanese captain's coordinate estimates for wind conditions, they could find him with all their airpower. I'm not trying to get you to wait. I totally understand why you want to leave in the morning. This new situation really is better, although very abnormal. We received six signals since late last night! That is unprecedented."

"What are you saying, Dr. Stern?"

"Angela, there are only three reasons this might happen. One is that the whale is swimming in such a way as to stay on the surface for a long time so that the waves are not covering the contacts. I think that is unlikely. Second, it may just be an amazing coincidence of mathematically phenomenal proportions. Third, your husband removed the transmitter and it is on his raft."

"Oh, my God." Angela could not contain her excitement.

"Don't get overconfident, Angela. Even if this tracking plot continues, it is not going to be easy to find the raft. The clock is ticking so anything can happen."

Angela thought about the options.

"Would you give me the number for MMS? I think that was the name. I want to leave in the morning. What do we need to track the whale or the raft?" Angela had regained her composure.

"I thought you'd make that decision. I've already

made arrangements for us to be in constant communication with the plane to update the coordinates. The only reason they were willing to leave in the morning is because the satellite shows the transmitter is less than 800 miles from Maui. That is about the halfway mark for their airplane."

Angela took a cab to MMS and arranged the next day's flight. Again she was told that everything depended on the weather.

The next morning was beautiful, although clouds appeared to the distant northwest. Angela, a pilot, navigator and two paramedics boarded a refurbished 1967 P5M-2G Marlin Sea plane. Although the airplane was well equipped Angela was taken aback by its age.

"This baby is better than what they build today. She cruises at 150 mph and has a range of 1,800 miles." The pilot spoke with pride and confidence. The entire crew seemed equally assured. All were aware of the seriousness of the project. This team had performed many rescues before. Even if the seas were too rough to touch down and pick up her husband they could drop a medic with supplies to support him until a boat arrived.

Last Song of the Whales

22. The Tanker

Brant didn't keep track of the days. He estimated he'd been at sea for two weeks, maybe longer. He knew that racing sailboats could make the journey from Victoria to Maui in 12 days. He didn't know it took the humpbacks between 22 and 30 days. At any rate, Boy was moving faster now, maybe five knots. It was almost too fast for the raft. For some reason he seemed to be in a hurry. Brant thought this was a good thing since he was going to run out of water no matter how carefully he conserved it. Eating the dorado hadn't helped his thirst. In fact it seemed to make it worse, although the blood undoubtedly helped him survive and the meat energized him somewhat.

Brant found himself talking to Boy now with the unquestionable expectation that he would understand the meaning of his words. As he reeled in the dorado, he exclaimed, "Look at it, Boy! Ain't it beautiful? Bet you would like this guy?"

After pulling the fish aboard, eating some and saving the rest for later, Brant fell asleep. When he wakened, he recalled a dream and began describing it as a poem in the style of his favorite poet, Robert Service.

"Hey, Boy," he yelled 60 feet ahead to Boy's ears. "Listen to this. Aristotle said dolphins like poetry. See how this grabs you."

It hurt Brant's throat to speak loudly enough so Boy could hear him over the sound of the waves slapping against the raft. He didn't know that Boy's excellent hearing would allow him to hear a softer volume, one that would have been barely audible to a human 10 feet away.

Brant began reciting a poem, constructing it almost without pause on the spot. It told a story of a man and a dog escaping together from a prison. For reasons unknown to him he had given the man the name, "Burlo Dundee." He went on with the poem as if in a trance, not knowing its source, or understanding his compulsion to create it, or to share it with the whale.

> There are legends of men with courage and pride,
> Whose passion it was to be free.

They loved with devotion and would stay by your side,
Such a man was Burlo Dundee.

Drunk in a bar with a friend he loved well,
Surrounded by mad men with knives,
Burlo knew it was war, when to the floor his friend fell.
Then he took from the mad men their lives.

From hate in a hurry, he was accused
Of murder in the first degree.
And with a rigged jury, he was not amused,
For it was life for Burlo Dundee.

He broke rocks in the dirt where he was confined
By a swamp instead of a wall.
And each step he took hurt for his leg dragged behind,
A chain and black iron ball.

One day faint and sweltered in the hot, heavy air
Was a hound pup gasping for breath.
Burlo brought him to shelter and shared his slight fare,
Saving the dog from its death.

When Burlo was fed, he'd give the dog half,
The guards all agreed it was funny.
When it shared Burlo's bed, all his comrades would laugh
At this fool named Burlo Dundee.

Burlo's loneliness dwindled as the dog grew and learned.
No truer friendship was ever fulfilled.
But now twice the dog had been kenneled
And twice it returned.
Now tomorrow it was to be killed.

For months he'd been filing (his friends thought it a joke)
With sharp stones on one link of chain.
While his thoughts kept him smiling, at last the link broke,
And the two disappeared in the rain.

His face was swollen red from the branches and bites,

Last Song of the Whales

And his eyes burned from sweat and the rain.
Though his feet and legs bled, through the days and the nights,
He kept on in spite of the pain.

The dog warned him of snakes and fought cats on the prowl
With a courage that would not falter or quiver.
The best trails he would take as he led with his howl,
Following scents that led to the river.

Then cold air from dry land touched Burlo's cheek,
And blindly he charged through the trees.
Soon he fell in the sand that he no longer need seek.
He was free as the great river's breeze.

As he lifted his eyes and regained his wind,
He looked all around for the dog.
Then he heard the cries, the call of his friend,
And he plunged back into the thick bog.

He followed the call, careful not to get lost
Knowing the hunters and hounds heard it too.
But in spite of it all, though his life it could cost,
His love and devotion were true.

The dog was deep stuck in a lake of quicksand,
But his eyes were still noble and brave.
Then the fatal shot struck as Burlo reached out his hand,
And joined his dear friend in their grave.

Having traveled so far with no proof to return
That the dog and the man were not free,
The guards lost their war with each man who would learn
Of the escape of Burlo Dundee.

Brant was quite amazed with how the words and the story came forth in rhyme without his having to take time to consider them. It seemed magical. He had never written a poem, though he had once memorized Robert Service's epic poem, "The Cremation of Sam Magee," which obviously had provided the meter for his poem. How he could have created such a long poem and such a unique story in only a few minutes, however, was beyond his understanding. As a writer, it would normally have taken him many drafts to pen it.

"Well, Boy, how did you like it? Somehow, I think it is about you and me."

Brant thought the poem's swamp must have been his dream's metaphor for the ocean and the hound dog was Boy. He, of course, was Burlo, trying to escape…from what? From the dangers of the ocean or something back in civilization? And did the dream poem prophesize his and Boy's deaths?

Night had arrived without him even noticing and the intensity of the stars was amazing. Equally wonderful was the light show in the water. Each time Boy's tail moved or slapped against the water, it ignited millions of glowing micro luminescent organisms in the dark water. The green, sparkling lights seemed like millions of diamonds energized with an internal lighting.

Brant was pondering such things when his SART

started beeping. The sound startled him. He thought the batteries would have been used up by now. He looked up and saw the lights of a huge ship bearing down on them. It wasn't more than two miles away and was rapidly approaching. It wasn't a cruise ship so he guessed it must have been an oil tanker. But it wasn't. It was Chevron's 1,200-foot by 220-foot Voyager. Although there was no way Brant could have known, the watchman saw the radar signal but ignored it, thinking it was insignificant. As it came within a half mile, Brant realized the watchman couldn't see him and had no plans of slowing down. Even worse, they were on a collision course with the tanker and Boy couldn't dive as he normally might because of the towline. Brant quickly released the line from the raft and yelled at Boy to dive. Boy stopped and turned back.

"Get out of here. That thing is going to run us over!"

Boy, once again acting as if he understood, turned and headed in a safe direction.

Brant started rowing the raft with all his might to get out of the tanker's way. He felt like an ant looking up at an elephant when it passed him. He was no more than 60 or 70 feet away when the stern when by. The huge wake lifted the raft up, spun it around and flipped him upside down. Brant climbed aboard the bottom of the raft, cursing the tanker with the slim hope that it saw him.

Boy returned while Brant was unsuccessfully trying to flip the raft upright. Boy swam underneath it and lifted it up on his neck. Brant climbed aboard the whale and managed to turn the raft over as he tossed it back into the water, right side up. He dove in the water and climbed back into it, desperate to see what he might be missing. To his great dismay, everything was gone except the pole, with its fishing line and hook, and the bayonet, which was wedged under the center pontoon. At least he could fish. He scanned the ocean and saw nothing in the dark night but he jumped off the raft and swam toward where he thought the boat had flipped. The oars, water jug and flare gun box might be floating there, along with the sail. He swam for 20 minutes, exhausting himself and then found his way back to the raft, thanks to the starlight.

He called Boy, who came instantly. Brant found the towline and reattached it to the raft. Brant was devastated. They would *have* to make good time now. He would not last long without water. If it didn't rain, Brant knew he could only survive two or three more days. He unfastened the fishing pole and threw the hook and plastic lure back in the water.

23. The Target Area

No sooner had the plane taken off when Loni's technician, with Loni at his side, radioed the pilot. They were looking at the charts, hoping for a clear track but something was wrong. He explained that sometime between 10 p.m. and 3 a.m. they had lost the signal. Loni got on the speaker and asked to talk to Angela. The navigator/co-pilot handed her his set.

Loni explained the situation.

"Angela, don't worry about this. It just means I was wrong about the transmitter being on the raft. It must have been on the whale, not Brant's raft. I'm sure we just hit one of those one in a million chances that each time the satellite was overhead the whale was on the surface. Now it's stopped, which means the whale is not surfacing in time to meet the satellite. That is normal. The pilots are going to head about 30 miles west of the last coordinate.

Hopefully that should put them within 50 miles or more of where the whale and Brant are. You should be over the area before 2 p.m."

Angela thanked Loni and handed the set back to the man. She looked at her watch. It was 8:22 a.m.

The hours passed slowly. By noon the sparsely clouded sky had been taken over by large cumulous clouds filled with water. The pilot announced they were ascending a little and would head back down shortly. Soon it began to rain and visibility diminished significantly. Angela cursed the bad luck in silence.

"What does this mean for our search?" she asked one of the rescuers sitting by her.

"Hopefully we will pass through it by the time we reach the search area. If not we'll still have a mile visibility, I'm sure. The pilot is really good at covering the ocean terrain at a low altitude so if he is out there we'll still find him."

Angela thanked him, closed her eyes and prayed.

The weather was still nasty, maybe even a little worse than before. It was 1:30 p.m. The pilot announced they were over the target area. Everyone asked to take their assigned observation positions and to "keep their eyes peeled."

The plane flew at a very low altitude. It was about 300 feet above the ocean. Searching every inch of water while looking out from her window, Angela tried to imagine Brant's despair. She knew he got seasick and imagined how horrible it must be for him on these rough seas. The plane made several 10-mile long passes, reconfirmed the coordinates with Loni's crew and continued the search. At 2:43 p.m. one of the paramedics shouted, "Whale ho at eleven o'clock!" Angela's heart stopped. The pilot banked slightly to port and then turned 180 degrees back. There was a group of about 16 whales, one of the largest they had ever seen traveling together in a migration, and they had seen a few. The pilot flew back and forth over the whales. Most of them dove as he got closer but several did not. They remained seemingly oblivious to the low-flying airplane. That also was unusual, the pilot noted. As he started to turn back again, Angela saw another whale by itself and told the paramedic next to her. He yelled to the pilot. "There's another one alone at four o'clock."

The pilot banked again, this time to starboard, and flew close to the whale. It was floating on its side and appeared to be dead. Perhaps the whales had just left it, he said. He looked back at Angela and spoke.

"The transmitter must be on one of them," the co-pilot/navigator announced. "No raft though and we only have another 20 minutes before we have to head back. The weather forced us to use more fuel than we planned."

They flew over the prescribed area for the next 20 minutes. Angela felt her heart sink as the airplane rose back to cruising elevation and headed back. She looked at her watch. Grief and hopelessness were dripping down her face in the form of saltwater tears. Through the blur she saw it was 3:12 p.m.

24. The Proximity

By morning Brant's wish for rain seemed possible. Storm clouds were gathering. By midmorning it was sprinkling, the wind was picking up and the waves were getting larger. The sun had grown warmer throughout the week, although it was still cool at night. Brant went most of the day with his dry suit unzipped and pulled down around his waist, along with his undergarment. He wondered if the suit could be used to catch the rain. Drinking from the bottom of the raft was aiding his survival but it was always salty. It mixed with the ocean waves that spilled into the raft and tasted like rubber. He took off the dry suit and stuffed his booties into the leg openings. His objective was to catch and store rainwater when the stiff rubber was held upright.

By early afternoon he was in the middle of a storm. Brant knew that Boy would have preferred to be traveling deeper underwater. Nonetheless, he was handling the 10-foot waves and the raft without any obvious trouble. The seas were far enough apart and not breaking in such a way as to flip it. Brant no longer feared what might happen. He leaned back against the bow and opened his mouth as wide as he could. The blisters on his lips cracked open and were bleeding. He was amazed at how, with so much rain pouring down, he only got a few drops at a time. His dry suit filled up quickly and he drank the overflow.

Lying there with the rain pelting against his naked body and his eyes closed, Brant listened to the wind, seas and rain. He was totally aware of everything around him. The idea that he was in the middle of the ocean being pulled by a whale no longer astounded him. Everything was as it should be. In spite of it all, including his slim chance for survival, Brant was content. Even if he couldn't save the world, he thought, today would be a good day to die. Then, as had happened with the poem about Burlo Dundee, he felt a poem come to his lips as if some source beyond him had written it and was using his mouth to read it.

"Hey, Boy, I think I got another poem for you," he

spoke softly.

> There was a man who would not rest,
> Until of his life he had made the best.
> When lost adrift in the open sea,
> He was glad at least that he was free.
> From the stars he had guessed his fate,
> But he had learned to navigate.
> Then to the east there flew some gulls,
> Toward the island of the cannibals.
> He stood perplexed amidst the tribe.
> With rings and coins he tried to bribe.
> But for his life they would not pay.
> The tribe would have them anyway.
> They stripped him bare as the fire grew.
> He knew for sure he'd be in their stew.
> In vain he prayed and yelled in fright,
> Then shrugged and said,
> 'Hope I taste alright!'

Brant smiled and shook his head. Perhaps he did not understand his new penchant for poetry, but he liked the meaning that one conveyed. Suddenly, his thoughts were interrupted by the sound of an airplane's engine. He sat up and listened more carefully. Yes. It definitely was an engine and it was low. The tanker must have reported his position. He looked up just in time to see an airplane several miles away pull into a steep climb. It wasn't any more than 400 feet above the ocean. Brant watched until it disappeared in the clouds. Maybe it will come back;

maybe not. One thing was certain. The plane was looking for him. He knew this intuitively. He also believed Angela was in it. So much for his thoughts about "today being a good day to die." He must see her again and tell her how much he loved her. He had to tell the world what the whales were doing and explain his theory as to why.

Although he seldom looked at his watch or cared about the time during the past days, something made him check it now. Without his glasses it was difficult to see the numbers without squinting, especially in the pouring rain.

It was 3:12 p.m.

25. Blood Brothers

Brant kept looking into the sky, waiting for the airplane to return. Two more nights had gone by. His dry suit water catcher had failed. The water leached out of the material, which obviously was not as watertight as he thought. It also leaked out past his booties. Some water remained in the folds, however, so he carefully tucked the suit in such a way as to store the remaining drops for future use. He was drinking what rainwater remained in the raft by placing all his weight on one end. He curled up in a tight circle and balanced on the pontoon, concentrating on his dwindling weight until the water trickled toward him. He leaned over awkwardly and sucked the salty rainwater until it was gone.

By the third day what water he didn't drink had evaporated. The sun was getting increasingly hotter. He had ripped off a leg section of his undergarment to make himself a stocking hat. It kept his bald spots from burning but it also increased the discomfort from the heat. Brant had thrown the uneaten portion of the dorado overboard when it started to smell. He kept several portions for bait. When Boy was resting, Brant could fish straight under the boat. He had nibbles but the fish managed to take the bait off the hook.

Boy seemed to be swimming with a purpose. The constant joy he usually emanated had disappeared since leaving the gyre. In fact, Brant thought he seemed depressed or perhaps desperate. Brant felt Boy's negative energy as strongly as he had felt the sense of peace, joy and harmony from him most other days. Brant supposed the whale was sick from all the plastic he had consumed.

The more Brant thought about his hypothesis the more sense it made. Whales were not trying to destroy the plastic nor inspire humans to do so. They wanted us to stop making the stuff, Brant said to himself. Damn. Something monumental was happening. The world had to know. The whales must be stopped before it is too late. How fast would the earth's atmospheric oxygen reach dangerous levels if half of the North Pacific whales died? How long would it take if whales from around the world were doing the same thing at the other four plastic vortexes?

Suddenly Boy stopped. He spy-hopped but did so with an obvious sluggishness that confirmed Brant's suspicion that he was sick. Brant glanced in the direction Boy was looking and listened. He heard whales. They seemed to be about three or four miles away but Brant heard them and so did Boy. Boy did not reply. He looked back at Brant with a sickening gloom in his eye and then, like a faithful sled dog, or perhaps like Burlo Dundee's hound, he resumed his task.

Brant was lying in the bottom of the raft when a large shadow passed over him. He looked up to see an albatross. Its wingspan must have been 7 feet and it flew directly over the raft, no more than 40 feet above him. Brant watched the great bird pass over. He knew this was an important message. He did not know the Indigenous meanings and teachings that related to different creatures but there was no doubt that this bird's appearance was significant.

He remembered Samuel Taylor Coleridge's famous poem, "The Rime of the Ancient Mariner," and how it described a sailor killing one of these remarkable birds.

He did not remember why the sailor did that. Brant did realize that the killing was an act of violence too typical of human beings who did not understand the importance of creatures beyond their usefulness to man. Brant admired Coleridge for making this point, if he indeed meant to do so. He knew colleagues who believed animals had no intrinsic value, only instrumental value for human purposes. Coleridge made it appear that the killing brought the sailor's ship bad luck, condemning the sailor to wander the seas telling his tale after his mates died. They all paid the price for disrespecting nature.

The poem reminded Brant of his many years of learning from traditional Indigenous Peoples. He had committed himself to this as a scholar but also as a way to reclaim his own Indigenous blood. What had he ultimately learned from them? He pondered this carefully, believing that now was the time in his life to understand whatever wisdom he had gleaned. A major aspect of the Indigenous Peoples' wisdom was about having respect for everything in nature. Rocks, rivers, insects, birds and fish were as important in the world as humans. In fact, most of these creatures were seen as potential teachers of man.

Next Brant thought about humor. Indian humor was at the center of most of the traditional people he had known, especially those far removed from Western culture, like the Tarahumara and the Seri. Humor got to the heart of things. He remembered the Hopi word for "clowning" was the same word for getting an important idea across to someone. Humor, like that in the famous coyote stories, offered contexts for deeper understandings about how everything is related.

When Brant thought about music it reminded him of Indigenous ways of being. All of the Indigenous origin stories he had studied told about the world being created with some form of music. Healing required singing, drums or rattles like most sacred communication. The whales and the Indians had a lot in common when it came to singing, Brant said to himself, as he thought about the Seri navigation songs again.

Balance also was an aspect of Indigenous world views. This was missing in Western culture. While thinking of this concept of balance, Brant thought about how Boy slept with one brain hemisphere fully operational and the other sleeping so he would not drown. This prevented the whales from drowning in their sleep.

Such complementarity between the two hemispheres must be far beyond where humans had fallen during the past 5,000 years. Brant laughed sarcastically at his choice of words. So much for evolution, he thought. People were de-evolving, it seemed, moving in ways less likely to promote species survival. Maybe the problem with humans was they weren't doing what was necessary to keep both hemispheres working together. (Brant noted that he had referred to humans as "they" as if he was no longer a member of this species.) Instead, over-emphasizing left brain-related functions dominated every activity. Even music was oriented toward success, power, money and competition for those who participated in it.

As a professor, Brant believed in the pursuit of truth as the ultimate goal for education. Truth and integrity was a vital life principle for most Indigenous cultures. It was essential for social balance and reciprocity. When first exposed to European lies, many elders thought those who told them were merely mentally ill and had no grasp of reality. Later they realized the lying was done intentionally. They knew that such a mind could easily be hypnotized by some singular authoritarian mandate, no matter how invalid. Brant considered that deception was at the root of Western culture's loss of balance and illogical, contradictory lives.

Brant recalled what his friend, Greg Cajete, a Tewa Pueblo Indian and fellow professor, once told him about Indian ways. He said that each individual is obligated to consider how differing energies, including those created as an aspect of actions, impact other beings' existence within the community. To have this perspective, one has to be aware of the invisible and visible energies. He said this awareness evolved from multi-level and multilayered symbols that originated when we could talk to the animals. The mediators for transferring this knowledge and reestablishing these basic foundations of balance were primarily the healers or medicine people. The most pronounced role was the shaman, who embodied the integration of relationships between humans and the more invisible entities around them.

Brant, thinking about the albatross again, sat up and looked for land. Night had fallen during his philosophical meanderings. He thought he saw the glow of a lighthouse in the distance when a petrel flew by. He didn't realize that's what it was. Even if he had he wouldn't have been able to identify it like he had the albatross. Nonetheless, he also knew that forces of nature were beckoning him to take action. He couldn't just lie there and wait to die.

In spite of his terrible thirst, he was too close not to have a glimmer of hope that he would survive. The thought that Angela was waiting for him reawakened his spirit. So, too, did his desire to tell the world about the whales and the plastic vortex. This, he thought, was the most important reason to survive. Surely, this close to land, some raft or plane would see him soon. Oh, God, please! There he went again with the "God" word. Yes. He was praying to something but it was too mysterious, too great for any human to describe. Brant was not asking this force to help him. Rather, he was acknowledging life and giving appreciation for it. By tapping into this force Brant remembered who he was and how he was connected to all things.

The night was almost over and Brant, delirious from hunger, thirst and the energetic contemplations of his mind, passed out. When he awakened, the sun had risen and was searing him with its heat. Brant's cracked lips were blistering more now. He searched for water ever so slowly within the folds of his dry suit. There was none. He knew he was dying. The dawn broke and he smiled at it. It would be the last one he would see if help didn't arrive soon. He wanted to appreciate it so he bathed his wretched body in its colors until they vanished and the white hot sun burned his eyes. He recalled his near-death experience when he was in the whale's jaws. Maybe he really had glimpsed the next world. It hadn't looked so bad. He hoped he might see the white light and hear the music again.

He thought about the whales and what they were doing. The idea that he was the only witness kept going through his mind. He believed he had, in fact, been selected to see it. He could not give up. As he thought this, a renewed strength soared through his dehydrated body and he sat up. The raft had stopped moving forward and Boy was floating still in the water, breathing shallowly. Perhaps he was resting. He could have been dying. It didn't matter. Brant looked at the great mammal and instantly knew he would have to hurt Boy in order to survive. Without hesitating, he took the knife in his teeth and pulled the line so the raft was just past the flukes. Once alongside the whale, Brant gently began cutting into his side, attempting to biopsy a two-inch chunk of meat deep enough to cause bleeding.

Boy remained still. "Easy Boy. This won't be so bad."

Brant had to go deeper than he wanted but Boy remained still. Soon bright red blood filled the four-inch deep hole. Brant placed his lips over it and drank and sucked for several minutes. He didn't hit an artery and after a while the bleeding stopped. He ate the small chunk of blubber and fell back into the boat exhausted.

Suddenly, Brant felt something move under the boat and the next moment he saw a large shark leap between the raft and Boy, ripping a section of meat from the whale just below the hole Brant had cut in Boy's side. Boy dove immediately. Fortunately the towline came off before it pulled the raft down. When he came back up, he did so with a vengeance and aimed straight for the shark. The shark turned and swam off but others surrounded the raft. Brant, moving on pure adrenalin, stabbed relentlessly at the creatures. Boy returned and the sharks disappeared.

"I'm sorry, Boy. It was my fault but I needed the liquid. Next time I'll make the cut higher on your back, OK?" Boy seemed to understand and resumed his resting on top of the water. In the distance, Brant could see land and his heart leapt. Brant, beyond exhausted, tried to think clearly. Boy could get him there inside two days if he continued pulling him but Boy seemed uninterested in continuing or was too ill to do so. In fact, he had stopped pulling the raft completely. Brant felt he was dying.

The current and wind seemed to be heading toward the land so Brant decided to take his chances. He might be washed ashore by nightfall. Maybe a boat would see him sooner. Time was wasting and every moment without water was crucial. He untied the towline, let it fall and said farewell to Boy as the wind and currents pushed him away from the sleeping giant. Conflicting thoughts and emotions invaded his head. He was leaving an injured friend to die. Maybe he could send a boat out to get him. What about the evidence of plastic inside of Boy? Would Boy come back after him if he was just taking a rest? Curling up in the bottom of the raft, he fell asleep.

Last Song of the Whales

26. The Dream

Angela hadn't left her hotel room for several days. She ate and drank very little. She didn't answer the phone, turn on the television or take a bath. It wasn't that she was unwilling to face the death of her husband for the second time. She felt a strange feeling creeping through her, as if her work here wasn't finished or as if her husband was not really dead.

Loni figured Angela had a right to her privacy but she did wonder why she was still here. She stopped trying to reach her after the second attempt. Akamu also called twice. Meanwhile Loni was pondering all of it, trying to make sense of what seemed senseless. What caused the tagged whale to move off course and into the area of the North Pacific gyre where the whales never went? What happened to the transmitter? How was it able to stay on the surface for so long and why did it suddenly disappear? If the man in the life raft wasn't Dr. Cormac where WAS he and who was in the raft? Why did a whale take a man into its mouth and possibly stay with him at least throughout the night?

Loni wondered about the whales the MMS search and rescue pilots saw from the airplane during their search that day. They reported that one was dead and several others appeared to be sick. She also was concerned with the increasing number of reports about beached whales. In the last month there were many whale beachings on the coast of India, South Africa, Australia, the Virgin Islands, the Canary islands, the San Juan Islands, the Mediterranean coastline and the Atlantic and Pacific coasts. Was there a connection between the beached whales and the ones the pilot saw?

While Loni was sipping coffee and tapping her pen on the desk in time with a tune playing on a radio down the hall, Akamu walked in.

"What are you thinking?" he asked.

"You know, Akamu. There are so many unanswered questions."

Akamu usually engaged Loni in small talk before getting to the point. This time he went straight to it. "I visited my grandmother last night. She sent word that I should come. She had a dream she wanted me to tell you about."

Loni knew the importance of this. Akamu's grandmother was a highly respected shaman. But why would she want Akamu to tell her?

"Grandmother dreamed of a half-man, half-whale 'Aumākua.'"

Loni knew that Aumākua were gods to the Indigenous Hawaiians. They could be anything from animals to rocks or humans. They were considered to be intimate members of mankind who served as protectors, healers and advisors. Their role was to counteract trouble. Sometimes they punished those who did not learn their lessons.

"Aumākua would turn the oceans red and the children would stop breathing," Akamu continued.

Loni reeled back in her chair. She had read enough about Hawaiian shamanism to respect its power. When she was very young, her father took her to ceremonies conducted by one, although she barely remembered. She took hula lessons after learning the hula originally was a system of shamanism. Loni realized that Akamu's grandmother knew the old ways. The new age movement had largely obscured the original teachings for the younger generation but the grandmother didn't forget. Prophetic dreams, such as the one Akamu related, were described with *'olelo huna,'* speech with secret meanings that emerged only when the receiver was in tune with the prophecy's invisible forces. Loni knew that many people, some enlightened and some wanting to be, had been coming to Hawaii for centuries to learn the art forms often used to convey such knowledge so they could return to their homelands to help heal their own people. The Hawaiian locals referred to this knowledge as "*po'o huna,*" meaning "mysterious, hidden, and invisible." In recent decades, people referred to it as "huna." Loni knew grandmother understood that dreams, their interpretations and what people did with them could influence nature and events. Loni, even with all her Western education, knew that dreams and visions were as valid a knowledge source as any scientific research. Believing so strongly in other ways of knowing, Loni had memorized the phrase, "*A'ohe pau ka 'ike i ka halau 'ho'okahi*" ("All knowledge is not taught in one school").

What Loni especially liked about the traditional Hawaiian wisdom was its emphasis on joyfulness. Loni

remembered another saying, "*He 'olina leo ka ke aloha.*"
It translated to "Joy is in the voice of love." Before the
European invasion every system of life on the island was
designed to experience and manifest such joyfulness.

There also was a sense of balance. Every ritual, every
act was measured according to how it maintained a
proper balance for all of life—past, present and future.
Moreover, none of the mystical information was secret
then. Even children had access to it. There was no risk for
misuse because of the balance, because the sun and the
moon were always present in all aspects of their life.

Although Loni knew many of the Hawaiian stories, it
was a Navajo one that best represented the balance of
solar and lunar energies. It told about twin heroes whose
very names represented these forces. "Monster Slayer"
represented the sun's powerful and direct energy. "Child
Born of the Water," the lunar twin, was softer and more
reflective. The two were on their way to fight the
monsters, which, similar to the Hawaiian stories,
ultimately live inside each person. When they came upon
the "Monster with the Long Arms" Monster Slayer placed
an arrow into the string of his bow and prepared to shoot
it from a distance. Child Born of the Water stopped him,

saying it wasn't safe.

"What do you expect us to do?" Monster Slayer asked.

Child Born of the Water replied, "I think the monster's arms are so long he will grab us before the arrow reaches its mark. I think we should sing to him instead."

Monster Slayer put his arrow away and the two brothers sang. The monster, never having been treated that way, let them pass unharmed.

Loni knew about the twin hero stories in Western cultures. Cain and Abel, Romulus and Remus, Hercules and Iphicoles, also possessed the solar and lunar differences. In these stories, however, the solar twin dominated or even murdered the other. This was the difference between the Indigenous cultures and the dominant ones, she thought.

"Why would she want me to know about such a dream, Akamu?"

"I don't know, boss." Akamu often joked and liked to call Loni "boss" if only to irritate her. This time, however, he was attempting to add some levity. He also felt the seriousness of the dream. "I really don't know.

She must think you'll know what to do with it. I think it has something to do with Mrs. Cormac's husband, don't you?"

That's all Loni needed, another mysterious question. On the other hand, maybe the dream was an answer to all the other questions!

Last Song of the Whales

27. Another Rescue

For the rest of the day and night Brant drifted closer to land. When the new morning arrived he saw a lighthouse on the northern-most point of a large island. Where was he? Why weren't there any boats? What island was this? The questions came and went and Brant returned to his trance-like, near-death state. Boy had not followed and Brant feared he was dying. He wondered if the great whale really was a male and wished he knew for sure now.

He looked over his shoulder again. He could make out the contours of the land. He thought he saw several kayaks not far from shore and an outrigger-type boat fishing off the island's point near the lighthouse. So near but yet so far. Brant knew he was not going to make it. The thirst was choking him and he felt the life force oozing from his body.

A mass of birds hovered over the area where Brant had left Boy in the distance. A number of shearwaters and gulls were also following Brant and schools of fish were making the smooth seas bubble from their activities. A school of dolphins swam underneath the raft. Brant's smile returned and he began chanting, weakly and nearly imperceptibly, some sacred syllables again. He could almost see the musical vibrations of the song drift upward. He felt his spirit rise out of his body also. In a moment, from a vantage point high above the raft, he observed the life and death below him. As had happened when he was first taken by the whale, Brant saw his life pass before him again and felt the same pleasant sensations. The sadness he had felt when he realized he could not warn people about what was happening lingered for only a moment then vanished. He and Boy had done their part, others would surely do theirs.

Then suddenly he was pulled back into his frail body as he felt some mighty force lift the raft out of the water. Brant was tossed out and belly flopped painfully into the water. A moment later he felt himself being drawn into the dark jaws of a whale. Boy was alive! He had come back! Brant fell back onto the warm tongue and managed a smile just before he fell unconscious again.

Last Song of the Whales

28. The Beaching

Loni received a call from Ensign Jim Perry, a member of the U.S. Coast Guard Search and Rescue Unit stationed on the Island of Kauai. Apparently someone came upon a beached whale with a man's arm hanging out of its half-open mouth. The on-duty dispatcher heard the initial report and called MMS. He knew the folks there and was aware of their failed search for a humpback and a man said to somehow be in its company. He told Loni he also had just received the okay from Washington to go ahead with the requested search for the man involved with the Japanese whaler. Apparently there was a warrant for Brant's arrest, too.

The MMS operator spread the word to Jerry Bruxwald, the MMS aircraft pilot involved in the air search for Brant. Jerry called Loni who immediately called Angela.

Angela heard the phone ring and jumped to answer it. "Hello."

"Angela, this is Loni. The desk clerk told me you were still there. I'm glad. They found your husband. He is on a beach near the Kilauea Point National Wildlife Refuge on the north eastern point of Kauai."

"Oh, my God. I knew there was a reason I was supposed to stay. How is he? Is he OK? Where is he? When can I see him?"

"Angela, I'm so sorry. I don't know yet if Brant survived. All I was told is that the initial report said a whale beached itself with a man inside its jaws. He had no other details. In any case the medics were dispatched."

Angela composed herself. "How do I get there? When can I see him?"

"I've made arrangements for a group of researchers from the foundation to fly with me to the Lihue Airport. Of course I have space for you. We are leaving right away. I'll pick you up in 15 minutes."

Loni hesitated a moment and Angela waited. Angela was speechless. She had been right all along and she suspected there was much more to learn.

"Angela, there is something going on here. It's much

bigger than you or Brant or the whale or my research. I'll try to explain as best I can when I see you but I don't even know exactly what it is. I just know that Brant has something important to tell us and we need to know what it is. I'm on my way to get you."

Last Song of the Whales

29. The Whale-Man

Boy selected a perfect wave and rode it just behind the crest to shore. He propelled his large body at the last second to beach himself beyond the surf line. An hour later, several children who had been collecting shells for making necklaces, spotted him and were even more shocked to see a man inside the creature's half-open jaws. The most athletic of the youths, a boy in his early teens, ran two miles back home to his fisherman father. Within minutes dozens of natives and a few beachcombing tourists were surrounding the remarkable scene. People were pouring water on the whale, passing buckets up and down a line of people that stretched to the sea. Others had gently removed Brant from the inside of the jaws. The whale and the man were both alive!

Within an hour, medical support was on its way via helicopter, as were Loni and Angela. The women landed on the scene while the medics were supporting Brant with intravenous medicine and nourishment. They did not want to move him until he was more stable. Angela ran to Brant and Loni ran to the whale.

Brant regained consciousness when he heard Angela's voice. Angela bent over and kissed his weathered cheek. "Everything's going to be OK now, honey. Your whale is alive, too." Angela did not want to tell him she had just heard someone say the humpback had died.

Brant was unable to speak but Angela knew he didn't believe her. She saw the pain in his expression just before he passed out.

30. Boy's Sacrifice

The whale died shortly after Loni reached him and just moments before Angela reached Brant. She had immediately ordered an autopsy that began after Brant and Angela were airlifted to the hospital. More than 10 square meters of plastic from the whale's stomach had been spread on the beach. Photographers from all over took pictures before everything was stored in canvas bags and the whale was taken back out to sea.

Before being released from the hospital, Angela and Brant arranged for Boy's funeral to be held on Christmas morning, nearly three weeks after Boy brought him ashore. Angela had called a select group of friends to come to the island for the event. If peace on earth was to be celebrated on this date, they could think of no greater opportunity. At 6:30 a.m. the Maui Coast Guard, who had motored their 47-foot response boat to the island the night before, picked everyone up and took them to a place just off the coast of Kilauea Point National Wildlife Refuge. It was near where Brant and the whale were discovered. Loni, Akamu and the MMS search and rescue crew also were aboard.

The Coast Guard craft anchored and they waited for the sun to rise. At 7:01 the distant red sky brightened with yellow hues until a white sun and blue sky emerged in its place. Loni looked out at the white beach along the shore. Plastic debris had started showing up several years ago. In spite of local complaints, not much was done to clean it up. Now it was virtually plastic free. When word got out about the nearly ten square meters of plastic garbage that had been removed from Boy's stomach, the entire community and people from numerous other islands arrived *en mass* to clean up the island's beaches. The town already had called an emergency meeting of the local government to consider outlawing plastic bags in stores.

Loni looked out and around the ship. It seemed like all Hawaii's native fishing boats were surrounding them. She saw traditional canoes, fiberglass kayaks, outriggers and modern fishing boats. In front of her, and at the head of the boat formation, was a traditional double-hulled voyaging canoe, a vaka taurua. In the pola, the seat between the two 50-foot long hulls, sat Akamu's grandmother. The canoe was beautiful and obviously made in the traditional manner. Its hulls were close together, bound only by rope lashings.

Making such a boat was a spiritual undertaking. For four days the Kalai Wa'a, the woodcarver, prayed for a suitable koa tree. Then he went into the koa forest and watched for an Elepaio bird to arrive. If the bird pecked at the bark of one of the trees, the carver knew it wouldn't be sound enough for the boat. Its heart would be decayed. This observation period could take days before the carver and his helpers were confident in the tree selected.

All of the craftsmen involved with making the canoe joined in sacred ceremonies relating to its completion and launching. Before setting the new canoe afloat they fished for a red moana. Upon catching the first one, the canoe's owner would eat the entire fish and return the bones to the sea.

Loni thought of the grandmother's dream. To bring such a canoe here had great significance. If only the world governments' decisions-makers had the same regard for what happened. Loni did her best to inform the newspapers and a worldwide network of marine and environmental scientists of her and Brant's theory. Brant had managed to share bits and pieces of his story while in the hospital and she had started making phone calls and writing articles well before Christmas arrived. She begged other scientists to investigate the world's gyres for unusual whale activity and to autopsy dead or beached whales when possible. She was working to get funding for an expedition to the North Pacific Gyre to confirm what Brant described. In short, she was doing everything she could to get the world to pay attention to Brant's story. Sadly, her efforts did not seem to be having much of an impact globally and it would be months before a peer-reviewed journal would publish anything, if they accepted an article for publication at all.

Loni withheld her belief that the whales understood all of this better than she did. She merely tried to show scientifically that if enough whales did indeed eat the plastic and were dying at sea, their decaying carcasses soon would add significantly to the process of ocean apoxia already creating worldwide dead zones. She wrote that the earth's global oxygen levels could be seriously affected if phytoplankton became unable to absorb carbon dioxide as a result of the rapid loss of oxygen in the water. The dead whales could tip the scales of a process already started by global warming, plastic pollution, industrial runoff and oil spills. She e-mailed it to everyone she knew and also posted it on the foundation's website.

Environmental groups and government agencies from around the world were reporting the story of Brant's adventure but most only focused on the remarkable fact that a whale towed him across the ocean. Only a few articles gave much space for this theory. She heard that some agencies even were attempting to secure funding for gyre exploration. Others planned more in-depth research about the harmful algae blooms. Her own foundation had authorized a boat to go to the western and eastern garbage patches. It was leaving the day after the funeral with Loni aboard. The international response, however, was not what she expected, certainly nothing to match the valiant effort of Brant and the whale. She thought of a painting she recently saw that was done by German artist Hans Rudolf Giebeler. It showed a group of gray haired men scratching their heads while discussing something important. Above them, unnoticed, the sky was on fire. Buildings were flying through the air and the oceans were being sucked up into tornados. In the painting's foreground, a lone woman was moving toward the men. One could not know without asking the artist if she was on her way to alert them and take action or merely to join their discussions, politics and arguments.

31. The Ceremony

Loni and the others watched as Angela tied ribbons to the whale's rib bone and dropped it overboard. The ocean was blood-red with another algal bloom. A child on the boat began wheezing until her mother squeezed some prescription corticosteroid inhalant into her mouth. She started crying, which let her breathe easier and lowered her anxiety. Again Loni thought of the grandmother's dream.

Once the whale bone hit the water, the boat was engulfed by a musical sound that stopped everyone in their tracks. From the many native boats, hundreds of Hawaiian Indigenous natives were wailing a deep-pitched lamenting chant or a ho'ouweuwe. Something about this song was different from other funeral songs Loni had heard. It was about awakening.

E ALA E

KA LAI I KA HIKINA

I KA MOANA

KA MOANA HOU HONU

PI`I KA LEWA

KA LEWA NU`U

I KA HIKINA

AE A KALA

E ALA E

E ALA E

Loni knew enough of the language to understand the words:

In the east, there is the sun, arise, awaken
At the ocean, the deep ocean.
Awake, the sun is in the east.
Climb to the heavens, highest heaven.
In the east, there is the sun, arise, awaken.

As the last of the long-held syllables echoed across the sea, there were gasps from those aboard as they saw hundreds of whales and dolphins encircling the boats and the ship. The native chanting vibrated out into the ocean and the singers stopped to listen. Another song, strangely similar, was echoing back to the humans. This one was from the whales.

Loni, Brant and Angela listened as tears flowed down their cheeks. They wondered if this would be the last song of the whales.

About the Author

Four Arrows (Wahinkpe Topa), whose Anglo name is Donald Trent Jacobs, is of Cherokee and Scots-Irish ancestry. He is also an Oglala Sun Dancer, having fulfilled his Sun Dance vows with Rick Two Dog's Medicine Horse Dance on the Pine Ridge Indian Reservation. With doctorates in health psychology and curriculum and instruction, he served as Dean of Education at Oglala Lakota College and was a tenured associate professor at Northern Arizona University. He is currently on the faculty of the College of Educational Leadership and Change at Fielding Graduate University.

Specializing in health psychology, critical pedagogy, sustainability education and Indigenous worldviews, he has authored 18 non-fiction books, including *Primal Awareness: A True Story of Survival, Awakening and Transformation with the Raramuri Shamans of Mexico* (Inner Traditions International); *Unlearning the Language of Conquest* (University of Texas Press); and *Critical Neurophilosophy and Indigenous Wisdom* (Sense). He also has authored numerous invited chapters for books on education, ecology and peace in addition to more than 100 journal articles, including the first multi-generational peer-reviewed article, "Anthropocentrism's Antidote: Rediscovering Our Non-Human Teachers," written with his daughter and grandson and published in *Critical Education* (UBC).

When he is not teaching or writing, Four Arrows enjoys whale watching, kayaking, sailing and handball. In 1996, he was first alternate for the U.S. Equestrian Team and his love for horses continues with his learning to play arena polo. He lives with his artist/photographer wife, Beatrice Angela, in a fishing village in Mexico during the winter and a fishing village on the west coast of Vancouver Island in the summer. Whales visit often in both places.

Last Song of the Whales

If you enjoyed *Last Song of the Whales* consider these other fine Books from Savant Books and Publications:

A Whale's Tale by Daniel S. Janik
Tropic of California by R. Page Kaufman
The Village Curtain by Tony Tame
Dare to Love in Oz by William Maltese
The Interzone by Tatsuyuki Kobayashi
Today I am a Man by Larry Rodness
The Bahrain Conspiracy by Bentley Gates
Called Home by Gloria Schumann
Kanaka Blues by Mike Farris
First Breath edited by Z. M. Oliver
Poor Rich by Jean Blasiar
The Jumper Chronicles by W. C. Peever
William Maltese's Flicker by William Maltese
My Unborn Child by Orest Stocco

Scheduled for Release in 2010:
Mythical Voyage by Robin Ymer
Ammon's Horn by G. Amati
Perilous Panacea by Ronald Klueh
Hello, Norma Jean by Sue Dolleris
Falling but Fulfilled: Reflections on Multiple Intelligence
by Zachary M. Oliver
In Dire Straits by Jim Currie
Charlie No Face by David Seaburn
In the Himalayan Nights by Anoop Chandola

http://www.savantbooksandpublications.com